Michelle Kwan & Tara Lipinski
Skating Champions

The music began. Michelle Kwan, wearing a flowing, red and gold silk costume, seemed confident and in total control. Gradually picking up speed, she jumped high into the air, completing a graceful triple lutz–double toe combination.

Tara Lipinski, wearing a white dress with gold trim, watched and waited. A bundle of nervous energy, she shifted restlessly from skate to skate as she stood on the mat-lined walkway to the ice.

Michelle and Tara were the final two skaters in the free skate program. There was only one question now—which one would end up on top? Both skaters had ambitious programs with seven triple jumps planned. How they executed each one would spell the difference between winning and losing. . . .

Here's the real up-to-the-minute story on Michelle Kwan and Tara Lipinski, in an action-packed two-in-one biography that takes you from the very beginning, when Michelle and Tara tried on their first pair of skates, to their rise to the top skating competitions.

Now Michelle and Tara are going for the gold. Here's your chance to get the insider's look as these skating superstars face the 1998 Winter Olympics.

SKATING FOR THE GOLD

MICHELLE KWAN & TARA LIPINSKI

CHIP LOVITT

AN ARCHWAY PAPERBACK
Published by POCKET BOOKS
New York   London   Toronto   Sydney   Tokyo   Singapore

AN ARCHWAY PAPERBACK *Original*

An Archway Paperback published by
POCKET BOOKS, a division of Simon & Schuster Inc.
1230 Avenue of the Americas, New York, NY 10020

Text copyright © 1997 by Chip Lovitt
Insert photographs copyright © 1997 by J. Barry Mittan

ISBN: 0-671-01679-2

First Archway Paperback printing October 1997

10 9 8 7 6 5 4 3 2 1

AN ARCHWAY PAPERBACK and colophon are registered trademarks of Simon & Schuster Inc.

Cover photo by A.P. / Wide World

Printed in the U.S.A.

IL 5+

Acknowledgments

The author would like to thank the following: Heather Linhart and the Communications Department of the U.S. Figure Skating Association for their help in providing all kinds of valuable information; Keith Lovitt for his assistance with research and word-processing; Julie Komorn for editorial support; the staff at the Danbury Public Library; and all the on-line figure skating enthusiasts whose Internet reports and opinions provided the fan's-eye view of the sport.

Contents

SKATING FOR THE GOLD

1

Tara's Triumph

Just about the same time in March 1997 that spring descended upon the picturesque city of Lausanne, Switzerland, so did more than two hundred of the world's finest figure skaters. The city, surrounded by the magnificent mountain peaks of the Swiss Alps on one side and beautiful Lake Geneva on the other, was the site of the 1997 Figure Skating World Championship, better known as the Worlds. Winter had just released its grip on the city, the "Olympics Capital of the World," and the mood was festive, thanks to the arrival of skating's biggest stars.

Billed as a battle of champions, the 1997 Worlds had drawn top-ranked skaters from the United States, Canada, Europe, Japan, China and many other countries. Despite the abundance of talent, most eyes and nearly all of the media's attention seemed to be focused on two sensational teenage skaters from the United States. One was Michelle Kwan, the sixteen-year-old defending world champion, and the other was her fourteen-year-old challenger Tara Lipinski, who in the previous month had turned the skating world upside down with two amazing upset victories over her older rival. As a result, the 1997 Worlds was shaping up to be a spectacular skating showdown.

Just a month earlier, 4′ 8″, 75-lb. Tara Lipinski had given the performance of a lifetime, dazzling audiences in Nashville, Tennessee as she wrested the U.S. title from Michelle, who fell not once but twice. Two weeks later, she outskated a still-shaky Michelle again at the Champions Series Finals.

Now as the 1997 Worlds were about to begin, the momentum had clearly shifted in Tara's favor. Suddenly she was more than just a contender for the world title. As the new U.S. champion, the young skater from Texas was, in many eyes, the favorite. The pressure was intense, although no one would know it from Tara's cool, seemingly carefree attitude and her ever-present smile. If she was at all nervous, it didn't show.

"Pressure? I don't feel that much pressure going into the Worlds," Tara said. "Last year I was fifteenth. I just want to get better than that."

Michelle's mood, on the other hand, was serious, and she was wracked by self-doubt. Just a year earlier, she had won the U.S. title, then dethroned world champion Chen Lu of China with a perfect performance at the 1996 Worlds. But in the month prior to the 1997 Worlds, she had suffered through the worst month of her skating career and was now experiencing a crisis of confidence. She had taken disastrous falls in the Nationals and Champions Series, and had lost her national title to Tara. Throughout her career, she had always been a sensitive and self-conscious athlete. With the weight of the Worlds, she seemed to have grown even more introspective. Being a world champion, and staying one, is a huge challenge, but it's even tougher when you are a teenager.

In the previous five years, no woman skater had managed to hold onto the world title two years in a row, and Michelle was more than aware of that fact. And since February, Michelle's chances of holding onto the crown looked as shaky as some of her recent jumps.

For Michelle, there was more to this Worlds than winning. She had something bigger to prove. "I want to show that I've still got it," Michelle declared. "This is like a fight. You need to be strong."

No one, of course, was counting Michelle Kwan out, least of all Michelle herself. One of the most artistic and athletic skaters in the world, Michelle believed she had become her own worst enemy. "I can't really worry about Tara," she said, "because at both competitions I beat myself. No one can beat me but myself.

"I've been skating not to lose more than to win,"

she added. "That's not how I won my championships in the first place. It's up to me to get my confidence back."

In any year, the Worlds is the highlight of the international figure skating season. But the 1997 Worlds was especially important. Less than a year away was the 1998 Olympics in Nagano, Japan. The 1997 Worlds would be both a springboard and a preview to the upcoming Winter Games. The last three women skaters to win Olympic gold—Katarina Witt, Kristi Yamaguchi and Oksana Baiul—had all won the Worlds the year before, and neither Michelle nor Tara needed a reminder.

Winning a world championship *and* an Olympic gold medal today practically guarantees a lifetime of fame and fortune and a place among sports immortals. Successful skaters can now easily make more than a million dollars per year from endorsements and appearances. Some say an Olympic gold medal in skating can mean as much as $10 million per year. So the stakes at the 1997 Worlds were as high as they get. Tara and Michelle both knew there was an awful lot riding on the outcome of this world championship.

And, as always in figure skating, it all rested on the most narrow of edges—a quarter-inch metal skate blade. For athletes like Michelle and Tara, competitive skating is truly a life on the edge—in more ways than one. Few sports require the kind of precision and power needed to perform moves like the triple lutz, which requires a skater to take off from the back outside edge of one skate while skating backwards, spin in the air three times, then land on the back outside edge of the opposite foot—all done while moving at fifteen to twenty miles per hour. In recent years, spectacular jumps have become one of the keys to winning competitions, and extraordinary skills and training are required to master them. While skaters such as Tara and Michelle often make the jumps look easy, no sport requires more, in terms of sheer athleticism and artistry, than figure skating.

And as Michelle had learned, when that narrow blade slips, the results can be disastrous. A fall, a single stumble, or even a less-than-elegant facial expression or hand gesture can cost a skater critical tenths of a point in a competition, and make the difference between being a champion and an also-ran. A perfect performance, on the other hand, can bring a lifetime of rewards. Michelle's falls had cost her the U.S. title. Now she worried what a fall at the Worlds might do to her hopes for a second world title.

Tara Lipinski met the press on Monday, March 17. More than 100 reporters showed up to catch a glimpse of skating's newest star, and a dozen camera crews jockeyed for position trying to get a better look. It wasn't until the 4' 8" skater climbed up onto a chair that most of the crowd could even see her!

Despite her recent victories and the fact that the momentum seemed to be with her, Tara's goals were modest ones. They had to be. Just a year earlier at the 1996 Worlds, she had been on the verge of being eliminated from the Worlds altogether after an awful first-round performance that left her in twenty-third place. She recovered to finish fifteenth overall, but having finished out of medal contention in 1996, she knew she had little to lose and everything to gain at these Worlds.

"It's fun for me just to be here. I'm not even expecting to win or even place. It would be nice to be in fifth or sixth place," Tara said hopefully.

Her coach Richard Callaghan also had modest goals for Tara. "I don't think she's going to win it," he said, "and she doesn't think she's going to win it. She certainly has a chance.

"If both Tara and Michelle both skate clean, Michelle will win," he predicted. "Michelle has had a couple of bad competitions, but I still respect her edge and experience."

The only thing Tara would promise was a more mature look and performance. "This year we have a more sophisticated program from last year. I wear my hair in a bun. My dresses are a little different," she offered.

"Michelle Kwan is not my rival," Tara added. "She's an idol of mine."

Michelle now found herself in the unusual role of underdog. Some suggested that Michelle's recent "growth spurt"—she was now 5' 2" and 102 lbs., two inches taller and five pounds heavier than the previous year—might be the cause of her recent jumping problems. "I don't know if it's the changing of my body," she countered. "I try to adjust as well as I can. It's been a little difficult the whole year. I just have to get my head straight and be more aggressive."

There were other threats to the throne besides Tara. Other contenders included Chen Lu, the 1995 world champion, European champion Irina Slutskaya, and the 1995 U.S. champion Nicole Bobek who, thanks to her new coach Carlo Fassi, was skating in peak form again.

No matter who was considered the favorite, nothing is guaranteed in figure skating—especially at the Worlds. As Michelle's coach Frank Carroll liked to say, "Anything can happen. Ice is very slippery."

The women's short program began on Friday, March 21. Tara was edgy and nervous all day. She always felt that way before a major competition, but the feeling was more intense because this was the Worlds.

The short program is a two-minute, forty-second performance worth one-third of the total score. A skater must complete eight required elements: double axel, triple jump, jump combination (two jumps without a step in between), flying spin, layback, spin combination, spiral step sequence, and step sequence. Missing just one element or performing just one element badly can result in lower marks.

There is a saying in skating that a gold medal can't be won in the short program, but it can be lost. If a skater has a disastrous short program, it's virtually impossible to make up the difference in the second program, the free skate. "In the short program, every move counts so much," noted Peggy Fleming, the 1964 world-champion-turned-commentator.

The Malley Sports Center in Lausanne was packed for the short program. Tara was scheduled to skate after France's silver medalist Vanessa Gusmeroli. Gusmeroli skated beautifully. Her scores were excellent and they put her in first place.

Tara was dressed in a short, sophisticated green velvet dress with tiny buttons and a white lace collar. Her light brown hair was pulled back in a bun. She walked down the mat-covered runway towards the ice, bouncing lightly on her skates. She was smiling, but she looked nervous.

Tara *was* nervous. She couldn't stop thinking about her disastrous short program a year earlier. Could it happen again? she wondered.

When she confided her fear to her coach, Richard Callaghan reassured her. "You're a different skater now," he told her. "You're ready for this. You've had a full year of training. Just do your work and it will pay off." Callaghan had one final piece of advice. "Please don't try to win," he instructed. "As soon as you do, you'll lose your focus. Just do your work."

As the music from the soundtrack of *Little Women* began, Tara gazed upwards, her arms extended like a ballerina. Looking both composed and in complete control, she picked up speed, then attempted a triple lutz, one of the most difficult moves in figure skating. Landing perfectly, she readied herself for her next move, a double loop. She took off, spinning her tiny body in tight circles. When she landed, she wore an exultant smile on her face. She knew she had performed it beautifully, and so did the crowd, who burst into applause. Tara danced across the ice, then launched herself into a polished triple flip. Judging from the grin on her face, Tara knew she nailed it.

Tara didn't get a lot of height on her jumps, but she didn't need to. She was able to spin so fast on her triples that she could complete three revolutions before landing. In the final seconds of her program, Tara ended her performance in the same pose she had begun it—hands and arms arching toward the sky, eyes cast upward. A joyful smile lit up the young skater's face.

"Wow" was all TV commentator Peggy Fleming could say.

Tara got a standing ovation from the crowd; many spectators waved American flags. Her first score for the required elements was an excellent one—5.8, from the French judge. Then came a lower one, a 5.5, from the Bulgarian judge.

"A 5.5?" Tara asked in disbelief. She grimaced, then gritted her teeth. Taking a sip of water, Tara sighed with relief as the rest of her marks—5.8s— were announced. A year ago at this time, Tara was in twenty-third place. Now she was in first.

Tara's marks were good, but there was still plenty of room for Michelle to take the lead if she skated perfectly. After all, this was the skater who had scored two perfect 6.0s to take the title away from Chen Lu at the 1996 Worlds. And Maria Butyrskaya, the four-time Russian champion, was about to skate.

As the Russian skater finished her routine, Michelle Kwan emerged from backstage. She wore a black velvet dress with sequins. Around her neck hung her good luck piece—a golden dragon pendant that her grandmother had given her years earlier. Looking beautiful, her hair pulled back and makeup elegantly applied, Michelle loosened up as she waited for the Russian skater's scores to be announced. When they were, Tara was still in first place.

There was a determined look on Michelle's face as she skated onto the ice. Until recently, she had been unbeatable, but the last five weeks had shaken her confidence. She seemed to have none of Tara's carefree ebullience. However, the time for soul searching, as Michelle knew, was over. As her music, "The Dream of Desdemona," by the French composer Massenet began, a subdued smile replaced the serious look on her face. The crowd gave a rousing roar to show their support.

Michelle's movements were graceful and polished, and she seemed in control as she glided across the ice. Moments later, she reached back and lifted herself off the ice in a triple lutz. She whirled three times in the air, then landed. The landing was shaky, and as Michelle stumbled, she threw in some extra steps before completing the combination jump with a double toe. It was a minor mistake, but an important one.

Michelle quickly regained her form. Her double

axel was flawless, her spins superb, and her connecting movements wove the rest of her routine into a fluid, seamless performance. Even her hand gestures—which judges look at carefully—were precise and elegant. As the music picked up, so did Michelle's confidence. She completed her triple toe loop without a mistake, then danced across the ice in a well-choreographed sequence that showed off Michelle's maturity and style. The music built to a climax and Michelle skated to center ice to end her program. She knelt down on the ice, then looked up with a smile as she acknowledged the crowd's applause.

Michelle knew she had skated well, and the relief that she hadn't fallen was evident on her face. But she was clearly upset about the triple lutz, and as she left the ice, a look of frustration and anger darkened her expression. She threw her arms down to her sides, her hands clenched in two tight fists.

Afterward, sitting at rinkside with her coach Frank Carroll, Michelle looked apprehensive. "I've waited so long for this," she said quietly.

Her scores for the required elements were good, but not enough to beat Tara's totals. Her presentation marks were better—mostly 5.8s and 5.9s. The totals, however, put her just below the top three. She was in fourth behind Maria Butyrskaya. Her shaky landing on the first triple jump had hurt her scores.

"It makes me so mad," she groaned after the short program had ended. "In warm-ups I did a great triple lutz. I do it all the time in practice. It's just one thing I missed out of so many in that program, and it's the one thing that counts the most."

Did she have to prove she still had it in the long program? she was asked. "I know I still have it, it's never gone," she answered. "I'm skating really well. Today just was a bad day."

Tara, of course, was quite pleased with her performance. "I'm extremely satisfied," she said. "Last year I had a bad short. And to be able to go out there and do a clean program was really great for me after last year."

The free skate was scheduled for Saturday and Tara was optimistic. "This gives me a lot of confidence," she said. "The last two competitions have given me more experience, so I feel more comfortable when I go out there. But you know, tomorrow is a whole new competition."

Tara grinned and showed off her newest piece of jewelry, a gold necklace that spelled out SHORT BUT GOOD. She had ample reason to smile. She was in line to become the youngest world champion ever.

On Saturday, Tara tried to pretend it was just another day. She and her parents went out to a little restaurant for some pizza. Then Tara went back to her hotel room. From her window she could see both the mountains and Lake Geneva and the view calmed her. For the next few hours, by her own account, Tara simply "vegged out."

The women's free skate is a four-minute program that is worth two-thirds of the total score. There are no required moves, and skaters must impress the judges with their artistry and technical skills. No skater can win a competition without a solid free skate program. "You can work all year, but your whole life comes down to one four-minute program in competition," Morry Stillwell, president of the U.S. Figure Skating Association, pointed out.

It was bright and sunny when Tara arrived at the Malley Sports Center on Saturday. Lugging her bags, Tara could have passed for a typical teen going to a slumber party, except for the crowd of camera crews that greeted her.

Vanessa Gusmeroli skated first in the free skate. Having placed second in the short program, she was now Tara's biggest threat. Gusmeroli lost her balance on her flip, but the rest of her program was solid enough to put her in first.

As soon as Tara stepped onto the ice, her nervousness disappeared. Dressed in a white dress with gold trim, Tara began skating to music from the movie soundtracks for *Sense and Sensibility* and *Much Ado About Nothing*.

Skating with assurance, Tara grew more confident with each triple jump she landed. Landings on triple jumps are always difficult, but Tara came down from her triple flip in perfect position. On her next move, a difficult triple lutz–double toe combination, Tara looked slightly unsteady on her landing, but she hammered her skate's toe picks into the ice to steady herself and successfully complete the move. Tara was beaming, and it was clear she was enjoying herself as she danced across the ice. She shifted into a series of layback spins, arching her back and throwing her head back while she whirled.

As the music shifted to *Much Ado About Nothing,* Tara performed a ballet on ice, then launched into a sensational triple loop–triple lutz. No female skater had ever attempted this combination jump in a world championship before, and when Tara landed it cleanly, the crowd went wild. The smile on Tara's face just kept getting bigger. The crowd began cheering even before she completed her final spins. By the time she finished, the crowd was on its feet.

Tara skated to the side, where she sobbed with joy and hugged her coach. When her presentation scores were announced, every judge had her in first place. Three more skaters followed Tara, but none of them succeeded in knocking her out of the top spot.

As Michelle waited to begin her free skate program, she looked relaxed, as if she had put her doubts and her falls behind her. Being the underdog had given her added incentive to do her best. As she would explain later, "The one who wins all the time is great and powerful, but the one who's been trampled, fallen, or been injured and is able to get back up and stand up and fight—that's who I admire the most."

At the edge of the rink, Michelle had a last-second talk with her coach Frank Carroll. "Attack," Carroll told her, "don't defend."

Michelle's free skate music—an exotic Eastern-flavored medley of "Gyulistan Bayati Shiraz" and

"The Love Story Behind the Taj Mahal" (the theme from the movie *Lawrence of Arabia*) began to play. It was a perfect complement to her costume—a red loose-fitting dress that made her look like the Indian queen she hoped to portray. Michelle completed her first move, a triple lutz–double toe combination, in fine form, but her next move, a difficult triple toe–triple toe, was the same jump that she fell on at the Nationals. This time she performed it beautifully and the crowd suddenly came alive. Michelle was again skating like a champion.

A tough decision lay ahead. Michelle was in fourth place, and playing it safe would not win a medal. She would have to keep the level of her jumps high and impress the judges with her control and style. Above all, her skating had to be free of any mistakes.

After a solid triple loop, Michelle danced around the rink, blending graceful circular skating steps with elegant hand and arm movements. She completed the performance with a superb double lutz and a triple salchow. As the music ended, Michelle made a final leap, then did a split in mid-air. The last-minute move capped what had been an inspired performance, and Michelle acknowledged the crowd's standing ovation by waving and throwing kisses to her fans.

Michelle was anxious to find out her scores, and so was Tara. Michelle's scores were excellent—even better than Tara's in the free skate. They were enough to put her into second place, but not enough to topple Tara. Had Michelle skated her short program as she had her free skate, she might have won the gold. Michelle had to settle for the silver, however she seemed genuinely happy with her performance.

"I just stepped on the ice and let myself fly," she said later. "It's a wonderful feeling to fly again."

Backstage, Tara sighed with relief as she heard Michelle's scores. She was still in first. But one final skater remained, eighteen-year-old Irina Slutskaya, the first Russian skater to win a European championship. Slutskaya skated well but failed to make it into the top three. Tara had finished first, followed by Michelle and France's Vanessa Gusmeroli.

Tara could barely believe she had won. "I never expected it, especially not this year. It's a big shock," she exclaimed happily. "But I love it."

Afterward, Michelle took tremendous satisfaction knowing she had risen to the challenge. "I really felt good," she said. "I just went out on the ice and said 'This is it.' I knew I'd worked really hard all year long for this. I had put a lot of pressure on myself, but now, it's like, this is nothing. I realized it's not life or death. Things haven't gone well for me this season," she added, "but today I got my act back together."

All three winners climbed onto the podium, clutching bouquets of flowers as they accepted their medals. Tara, wearing the gold, looked tiny on the podium, but her smile was a mile wide. In the stands, Tara's parents Jack and Pat Lipinski stood as the "Star Spangled Banner" was played and two American flags were hoisted to the ceiling. Happy tears streaked Pat's face.

It was a historic moment. At fourteen, Tara had become the youngest world champion ever, breaking a mark set in 1927 by Sonja Henie, who was fifteen at the time. Suddenly, the event in Lausanne had been transformed from a competition to a coronation, and Tara Lipinski was the sport's newest queen. And thanks to a recent rule requiring a skater to be at least fifteen to compete in the Worlds, Tara's place in the record book was assured forever.

Michelle wore the silver medal around her neck and a serious expression on her face. But when the crowd broke into wild cheering as the national anthem ended, Michelle began to smile. As she would say later, "The sun broke through again."

Although the 1996–1997 season had now ended, it was just the beginning for both Tara and Michelle. The quest for the ultimate prize and the crown jewel of competitive skating—an Olympic gold medal—lay ahead.

2

On the Move

When Tara Lipinski was born on June 10, 1982, in Philadelphia, her father Jack was somewhat relieved that he and his wife Pat had had a girl. Jack had played sports when he was growing up, and he knew that boys faced all kinds of pressure to be competitive, to be best in sports. Jack figured his daughter Tara wouldn't have to worry about that. Or so he thought.

"I ended up with more than I bargained for," Jack would joke many years later. Pat and Jack must have gotten a hint of things to come when Tara was seven months old. By that time, Tara was already on her feet and walking.

The road to a world championship is a long one, even if you're only fourteen years old. For Tara

Lipinski, it all began with a Care Bear and a pair of roller skates.

In 1985, when Tara was three, Care Bears were the rage. Every toddler, Tara included, wanted one of the cute and cuddly toy bears. One day while reading the local newspaper, Tara's mother Pat noticed an ad for a nearby roller skating rink. In addition to offering lessons, the ad mentioned a Care Bears giveaway. Pat called one of her friends who had a daughter Tara's age, and the four of them rushed to the rink in hopes of getting a free bear. When they got there, they learned the bears were free—but only with ten paid skating lessons. The two mothers reluctantly signed up for the lessons.

As Pat began lacing up her daughter's roller skates, Tara burst into tears. She didn't like the feel of the skates on her feet. But after Tara saw another toddler roller-skating, she calmed down.

"Tara doesn't like to see anyone do something she can't do," Pat Lipinski remembers. "Tara said, 'Put them on,'" and her mother did. Pat's friend took Tara by the hand and led her onto the rink. Tara's first steps were tentative, but as she got used to the skates, she began putting one foot in front of the other. Soon she was rolling along happily. It was clear Tara had talent, and by the end of her third class, her teachers were recommending private lessons.

"They saw something I didn't see," Pat recalled. Within a year, Tara was taking private lessons on a daily basis, and she impressed her teachers with her fearlessness and energy. When she was five, she began playing roller hockey with the local boys, some as old as eight and nine. "And she just kept winning," Pat said.

Pat and Jack were impressed with Tara's talent, but until then they had never expected their daughter to become very involved with sports. While Jack had played soccer and lacrosse in school, he didn't consider himself a serious athlete. Pat wasn't into sports at all, so neither Jack nor his wife thought Tara would have any major athletic ambitions.

"There were no huge aspirations," Jack mused. "There was no thought she'd be doing the things she is doing today."

The family settled in Sewell, a town in southern New Jersey. As a toddler, Tara attended Gymboree, a program that combines day care with play/athletics. Even then, people noticed Tara had above-average abilities. "We were there for three months," her mother said, "and the teacher said she had promise."

Tara took up ice skating at age six at South Jersey's Echelon rink. At first she fell a lot and "was flopping around all over the place," Jack reminisced. "She'll never be an ice skater," he had whispered to his wife. "Then Pat and I went inside for some hot chocolate. By the time we came out, Tara was doing exactly the same things on ice she could do on roller skates."

"Tara transferred everything she knew from roller

skating and was doing jumps and turns on the ice," her mother remembered.

Skating was more than just fun for Tara. By age six, she says "I realized that this was my life, that this was what it was going to be."

Tara spent weekend mornings at the roller rink and afternoons at the local ice skating rink. She entered roller skating competitions in both speed skating and artistic skating. By age nine, Tara was a national roller skating champion in her age group.

The family was living in Delaware when, in 1991, Jack took a job with a Texas-based oil company and moved the family to Sugar Land, a Houston suburb. Tara continued ice skating and roller skating for a total of four hours a day. Pat Lipinski, however, was worried that her daughter was not leading a normal child's life. After much discussion, Tara's parents decided that Tara should focus on ice skating and quit roller skating. There was more career potential in ice skating, they decided.

Tara was distraught at first. She cried for months and had hysterical fits of anger. To distract her, Jack and Pat tried to get Tara interested in baton twirling and other activities. Her parents set up a basketball hoop, hoping Tara would take up that sport, too.

Tara lists all the activities she tried. "I did horseback riding, tennis, gymnastics, modeling, ballet and jazz. They didn't last long. I quit baton twirling after the baton hit me in the head. And in gymnastics I didn't like doing flips, so that was a problem."

Jack and Pat even purchased a horse for Tara. She was such a good rider that she entered and won several rodeo competitions.

"She loved that horse," her mother said. "She would spend every Saturday and Sunday in the stable with that horse." But the cost of owning a horse was too much for the Lipinskis. "We told Tara she would have to choose between skating and the horse. We were sure she'd choose the horse. She said 'I'll take ice skating.'"

Tara immersed herself in the sport. She began entering competitions and was so busy with skating that she didn't have time to attend dances at the local country club or the birthday parties to which her friends invited her. Some of Tara's classmates didn't understand. They sent Tara nasty notes saying they didn't want to be her friend if she liked skating more than them. Tara was unfazed. She wanted to skate and that was all there was to it.

And skate she did. She got up as early as 3:00 A.M. and skated at the Galleria Houston Ice Skating Club before school, then returned to the rink when classes were done. She began working with a coach, Megan Faulkner, who was immediately impressed by Tara's love of skating. According to Faulkner, it was difficult to get Tara off the ice, and no matter what the activity—freestyle lessons, public sessions, or just practicing jumps over and over—Tara loved every moment she spent on skates. Even when she fell, Tara seemed to enjoy herself. Tara saw it all as a challenge.

It was apparent that Tara had far too much talent for the Texas skating scene. If she was to make progress, she would need more coaching, better skaters to learn from, and a larger rink. So in June 1993, just weeks after Tara's eleventh birthday, the family moved to an apartment in Elkton, Maryland, and Tara began training at the University of Delaware, a top-notch training site. She also got a new coach, Jeff DiGregorio. In order to pay for the coaching, the training and the ice time, Jack knew he had to keep his job in Texas, so he and Pat reluctantly agreed to live apart.

"It's not the greatest situation," Pat commented, "but we try to find ways to make it work."

"We decided our family needed roots, so I stayed at our new house in Houston," Jack added. "This way, we always would have a place to call home." However, like many skating families, the Lipinskis had to refinance their home in order to pay the skating bills.

Tara's daily routine consisted of five 40-minute skating sessions a day, six days a week. She also had instruction in ballet and a weight training regimen. It became clear to the Lipinskis that there was no way Tara could balance regular school and skating, so after her sixth-grade year, she began in-home tutoring for several hours every day.

During the summer of 1993, Tara began trying to master a new jump, a triple toe loop. A triple toe loop is a jump in which a skater takes off and lands on the same back outside edge and spins three times while in the air. Tara practiced it endlessly that summer and fall. In just a year, the hours of practicing those triple jumps would pay big dividends.

The skating life was not easy on Pat, whose day revolved around driving Tara from rink to rink, lesson to lesson, and watching and waiting in cold arenas. Pat toyed with the idea of asking Tara to quit, but she realized Tara loved skating and that it would be the worst thing for her if she were forced to quit. Pat could see that Tara was never happier than when she was skating. Whatever sacrifices she and Jack would have to make, they could not stand in the way of Tara's hopes. Someday, they wished, all of Tara's dreams would come true.

The year 1994 brought Tara all kinds of rewards and recognition. In order to compete in a U.S. championship, a skater must rise through the ranks in both regional and sectional events, first as a junior and then as a senior skater. Tara's climb was a quick one. In the novice, or youngest, division, Tara finished first in the Southwestern and Midwestern regionals, then finished second in the National Novice competition. She had begun to master her triple jumps, including the triple toe loop she'd first done the previous summer, and the jumps helped boost her scores.

While future rival Michelle Kwan would attend the 1994 Winter Olympics as an alternate, Tara had to content herself with watching the Olympics on television. At that point Tara could only dream of skating in an Olympics, but she could see herself someday standing on a podium winning a medal. She took three large Tupperware bowls from a kitchen cupboard and turned them upside down in front of the TV in her living room, creating a makeshift podium. Every time there was a medal ceremony and Tara heard "The Star Spangled Banner," she would climb onto the biggest bowl and pretend she was winning a gold medal. (This story has been reported many times. Some versions have Tara acting this out as a two-year-old watching the 1984 Games, while other accounts have her watching Katerina Witt win a gold medal in 1988. However, in 1997 Jack Lipinski said the incident really happened when Tara was twelve.)

In the summer of 1994, Tara burst onto the national scene when she appeared in the Olympic Festival in St. Louis. She wasn't originally invited to the event, but when Michelle Cho dropped out, Tara got the nod. She traveled to St. Louis, visiting the Gateway Arch along the way before arriving at the St. Louis Arena, the site of the competition.

Even as a twelve-year-old, her jumps were impressive. Wearing a teal dress with gold trim, Tara impressed the audience and judges with a triple loop–double loop combination in her short program. Thanks to her spectacular jumps, she finished first in the short program, ahead of several more experienced skaters.

And there was more at stake than just a gold medal and $5,000 in prize money.

"Whoever ends up on the podium will be going to

the Junior World Championships in Budapest, Hungary in November," said Carol Heiss Jenkins, an Olympic-champion-turned-coach, the day before the free skate.

The next morning Tara's coach Jeff DiGregorio was more excited than usual. "I had a dream about you last night," he told Tara. "I dreamed you skated a clean program and got a standing ovation when it was over."

In her free skate program, Tara skated to the music of *Samson and Delilah,* and she executed a smooth series of triple jumps. When the music stopped and Tara took her bows, she was amazed to see the entire crowd on its feet giving her a standing ovation. She waved to the crowd and smiled with delight. "I had no idea they were going to do that," she said later.

Tara won the gold medal at the Festival, becoming the youngest athlete to do so. She won the Mary Lou Retton Award and received the medal from the Olympic champion herself. It was then that Tara decided what her career goal would be. "My biggest dream," she said, "is to win at the Olympics."

Mary Lou Retton got most of the attention at the award ceremony, but Tara was happy just to be close to an Olympic champion. She and her family were also pleased with the $5,000 prize money. "You have no idea how much we appreciate that," Pat told the press. "One costume she wore here cost $600."

At a press conference, Tara's coach was asked how Tara had mastered her triple jumps at such a young age. DiGregorio had a ready answer. "She's very talented and has an amazing ability to rotate in the air very quickly. And she works harder than anyone I've ever seen."

"I just wanted to do the best I could," Tara said modestly. "I was very happy after I landed each triple toe loop. I've only been doing the triple since last summer."

Tara's small size, her smile, and her cheerful personality not only charmed the press but also endeared her to her fellow skaters. Tara spent most of the press conference sitting in the lap of sixteen-year-old Chrisha Gossard, the second-place finisher in the short program. "She's like a little sister," Gossard gushed. "I love her."

The fact that a twelve-year-old could capture the gold medal competing against so many more experienced athletes struck many observers as nothing short of incredible. Leroy Walker, president of the U.S. Olympic Committee, joked with Tara, saying, "I have things in my refrigerator that are older than you. It's amazing."

Besides winning a trip to the 1995 Junior Worlds, Tara got another treat on her way home. Mary Lou Retton lived in Houston, too, so Tara was able to spend some time with the champion gymnast. "I got to sit next to Mary Lou on the flight. She's really neat," Tara enthused.

Back in Texas that summer, Tara suddenly was a celebrity. Houston gave her the key to the city, and the Astros baseball team invited her to the Astrodome to throw out the first ball at one of their games. A banner with her name on it was hung at the Galleria Houston Ice Skating Club. Tara's feat at the Olympic Festival also attracted national attention, and the media was hot on her trail. She was profiled in a long *New York Times* article, and another paper dubbed her "the wonder kid." Soon after, a camera crew from *Good Morning America* arrived at her training site to interview Tara and Pat.

Tara enjoyed the attention, but she was more excited by the invitations to other skating competitions that flooded in. She was asked to participate in the Nebelhorn Trophy and Blue Swords competitions in Europe, and the World Junior tryouts as well. Tara was especially excited about getting to stay in the dormitory rooms with all the other skaters. It was the first time Tara had been allowed to be away from her mother and hang out with other skaters. While on her own, Tara did her hair and makeup by herself and she loved every minute of it.

Tara and her mother flew back to Texas to spend Christmas 1994 with Jack. Tara was supposed to spend the whole week in Texas and fly back to Delaware after New Year's Day. She loved being together with both her parents, but two very important events lay ahead: the 1995 World Junior Championship and National Junior Championship. The push was on and Tara didn't want to miss any of the training program she'd begun at the University of Delaware. So she convinced her parents that instead of a Christmas gift, they should buy her a round-trip ticket back to Delaware. Tara hopped on a plane, skated for five days at the university, then flew back to Houston to spend the New Year's weekend with her parents.

"Is this kid driven or what?" Pat was heard to say.

The California Kid

Compared with the nomadic life Tara Lipinski has led, Michelle Kwan is a relative homebody. She was born on July 7, 1980, in Torrance, California, and today she still calls the Orange County suburb her hometown.

Michelle's father Danny and her mother Estella had both emigrated to the United States from Hong Kong in the early 1970s. Upon their arrival in America, they settled down in southern California and worked in the family-owned restaurant in Torrance, The Golden Pheasant. The Kwans had three children: Ron, who was born in 1976; Karen, born in 1978; and Michelle.

Ron Kwan played ice hockey, and five-year-old Michelle liked to watch him skate. So did her older sister Karen. The two sisters decided that they wanted to take up skating, too. But at first, only Karen was allowed on the ice.

"My parents said I was too young," Michelle remembered. "They thought it was too dangerous." However, Michelle insisted on joining her sister in skating lessons, and soon Estella was shuttling all three kids to the local ice rink. Like many kids, Michelle got her start skating at a rink at a shopping mall. "My first skating memory," Michelle recalled, "is from when I was six. I was wearing skates and eating Nerds candy."

In the beginning, Michelle, by her own admission, was "shaky." She spent most of her time "falling on the ice and holding on to the rail like normal people." But it soon became apparent that Michelle had more skill than most and that she had both the physical and mental abilities to compete seriously.

By the time she won her first competition at age 7, Michelle had developed an intense desire to win. In 1988, she was watching the Winter Olympics on TV and saw American skater Brian Boitano win a gold medal with a series of spectacular jumps. As she watched the two-time world champion, Michelle was inspired by his style and was determined that she would learn to jump like Boitano.

Michelle has never forgotten that moment. "The first time I watched the Olympics on television I knew I wanted to be there someday. I thought I could just go there, like okay, tomorrow I'll go to the

Olympics." Years later she would discover just how difficult it is to make it to the Olympics.

When she was ten, Michelle's grandmother gave her a special good-luck pendant of a golden dragon. Michelle has worn it ever since. Not long after, Michelle was helping out at the family restaurant when she cracked open a fortune cookie. Michelle's eyes lit up as she read the message: "You are entering a time of great promise and overdue rewards."

Both Michelle and Karen showed such promise as skaters that the Kwans decided it was time to step up their training. In 1990, the two girls began skating for the All Year Figure Skating Club in Culver City and the Skating Edge rink in Harbor City, and putting in even more training time at the Blue Jay Training Center in Lake Arrowhead.

In 1991, a Kwan made it to the Nationals in Minneapolis, but it was Karen, not Michelle. While Karen skated against the likes of Nancy Kerrigan, Tonya Harding and Kristi Yamaguchi, Michelle had to content herself with being a spectator and practicing on a small outdoor rink.

"Michelle was furious," Danny Kwan remembered. "She kept saying, 'I'm never doing this again. I'm not coming to just watch.'"

That year, Michelle and her family decided it was time for her to begin training full-time at a single site. Michelle left home and the Peninsula Intermediate School in Torrance and moved into a small, rustic cottage at Lake Arrowhead International Ice Castles Training Center in the mountains 150 miles east of Los Angeles. Karen, too, joined her sister there under the tutelage of veteran coach Frank Carroll, who had worked with two-time world champion Linda Fratianne and Olympic medalist Christopher Bowman.

The move put a major financial and emotional strain on Michelle's family. While Michelle's mother stayed in Torrance to work at The Golden Pheasant, Danny worked full-time as a phone company systems analyst. He would drive two hours each night to Lake Arrowhead to spend the evening with his daughters. Then the next morning, after watching his daughters skate, he would drive two hours back to his job in Los Angeles. It was a grueling routine, and an expensive one.

Between Karen and Michelle, the Kwans were spending $50,000 to $60,000 per year on coaching, ice time, costumes, travel to competitions, choreographers, and all the other expenses young skaters struggle with before they break into the big money. By 1993, the expenses had ballooned so high that Danny and Estella had to sell their house in Torrance to pay the bills. They got more than $355,000 for the house, and they proceeded to pay off all their daughters' figure skating debts and bills. When they were done, they had just $600 left.

Later Michelle and Karen won scholarships from the Ice Castles Foundation, but it barely put a dent in the huge expenses the Kwans faced trying to keep two aspiring skaters in training.

The Ice Castles Training Center was an ideal

setting for the two young skaters. Nestled amid snow-covered mountains dotted with tall pines, the center is one of the top skating facilities in the country, and one of the most beautiful. Skaters train on a large indoor rink lined on one wall with tall mirrors that allow them to study their moves. The opposite wall boasts large picture windows that look out over the mountains. At the center, Michelle and Karen could focus on their skating surrounded by other top skaters and some of the sport's best coaches and choreographers.

In 1992, Michelle began her climb up the junior ranks. In one of her very first major competitions, she won the Southwest Pacific Junior sectionals and took third place in the Pacific Coast Juniors. Her showings in these events were good enough to win her a trip to the National Junior championship, where she came in ninth. Michelle was disappointed with her finish and knew she could do better.

The 1994 Olympics were coming up and Michelle watched with envy as skaters like Nancy Kerrigan and Tonya Harding competed for spots on the American team. As a junior, Michelle would not be eligible to compete in the 1993 Nationals as a senior, and thus could not be considered for an Olympic spot. As a result, Michelle was desperate to make the jump into the senior division. There was just one problem: Michelle's coach Frank Carroll did not want Michelle to become a senior. He was convinced Michelle needed more seasoning and that she should stick to the junior division for one more year and try for a gold medal at the 1993 National Junior Championships. Twelve-year-old Michelle had another idea in mind.

One weekend Carroll left town to attend a coaching conference in Canada. Michelle told her father that the qualifying test for southern California skaters to become senior-level skaters was coming up and she wanted to go for it.

"Ask Frank," Danny responded. Michelle had just one thought and it was to be a senior skater like her heroes Kerrigan and Harding. "I wanted to go up and see and compete with the big people," she later recounted.

A few days later, Michelle told her father that Carroll had said it was okay. Danny had no idea his daughter was lying, so he drove Michelle to the test, which required a skater to perform a four-minute-long program. The test demanded far more advanced moves and jumps than most junior level skaters can do, but Michelle passed easily. She was overjoyed. Her coach had a different reaction.

When Frank Carroll returned and learned what Michelle had done, he was quite upset. "I was furious," he recalled. "I sat down and told her I was captain of this ship and I would decide who were the mutineers."

Carroll was convinced that Michelle had plenty of talent but that she lacked critical artistic elements in her performance—skills that would only come with experience. At that time, he would later recall, "Michelle had no performance ability or showmanship." Carroll soon accepted Michelle's decision, but he kept reminding her that the two of them now "had their work cut out for them."

Michelle was now eligible for senior skating competitions. She could not return to the junior level except to skate in the World Junior Championship.

In retrospect, Michelle's instincts were right. In 1993, in rapid succession, Michelle took first in the Southwest Pacific Senior and the Pacific Coast Senior events. Michelle's photo graced the "Faces in the Crowd" column in *Sports Illustrated* magazine. Many observers, including her coach, recognized that underneath Michelle's sometimes shy demeanor, she had the strength, skills, and determination to become a great skater. She was, as one writer put it, "a flower with steel inside." With more training, Carroll was convinced that Michelle could easily compete with the best senior women skaters. Skating with seniors was no different than skating with juniors, Carroll said. "It's nothing," he told Michelle over and over.

Michelle's routine was grueling. Up at 6:45 A.M. for breakfast, she was on the ice by 7:45. From 9:30 till noon, she did schoolwork. After lunch, there was a second skating session from 2:00 to 3:15, followed by an hour-long nap. Then it was back on the ice for another session lasting from 4:30 to 5:20. Following dinner, Michelle began a weightlifting and cardiovascular workout that lasted another hour. By the time 8:00 P.M. rolled around, Michelle was often more than happy to go to bed.

For a short period of time Michelle attended seventh grade at a local school, the Mary Putnam Henck School in Lake Arrowhead. However, it was tough to balance a day in school with a practice regimen that required as much as six hours on the ice. Michelle, a good student, had a 3.5 grade point average, but she soon decided that she needed more lessons from her coach, so she decided to do independent studies. Once a week her teacher would arrive at her cottage and deliver the week's assignments and collect her completed homework.

What limited free time Michelle had she spent with Karen and other skaters. She and her sister often hung out at the Lake Arrowhead dormitory, talking, comparing their collections of pins and stickers, and watching an occasional TV show together. Each night the two girls eagerly looked forward to their father's visits.

At age 12, Michelle qualified to skate in the 1993 National Senior championship in Phoenix, becoming the youngest skater to participate in the event in twenty years. The pressure was tremendous, and Michelle did her best to deal with it. But under the surface, the strain was beginning to show. On the night before Michelle's first appearance in the championship, Danny Kwan was pacing up and down the hallway of the hotel, wondering how his daughter would do. He peered into her room, only to hear her mumbling in her sleep. "It's nothing. It's nothing," Michelle kept repeating.

Danny started to cry. He wondered if the demands of competitive skating were becoming too much for his daughter. Was Michelle being pushed too hard? The next day he and Michelle had a heart-to-heart talk.

"You are my daughter," Danny said softly, "but when I see you get stressed-out like this, I think it's time to quit. I just want you to have fun, to enjoy skating," he told his daughter.

Michelle, however, had no intention of quitting. She felt sure she could handle the pressure and wanted the chance to compete in the Nationals.

Danny was relieved, but he tried to give his daughter a sense of perspective. "I had to ask what this is all about and my answer is the one I gave her. Figure skating is a sport. It is not life. The lessons she learns now will be important to her in the future. Work hard, do your best, learn how to step up as a winner, and how to take defeat. Those are lessons for life," he advised Michelle.

Michelle convinced both her father and her coach that she deserved to skate in a national championship when she finished a respectable sixth out of twenty in the 1993 Nationals. Landing four triple jumps—more than any of the top contenders—twelve-year-old Michelle proved she was more than worthy of competing at the senior level.

In April 1993, the U.S. Figure Skating Association

chose Michelle to represent the United States at the Gardena Spring Trophy Championships in St. Ulrich, Italy. The association's faith in Michelle was not misplaced. She finished first.

But the highlight of the year for Michelle was the 1993 Olympic Festival in San Antonio, Texas, that summer. The weather was hot and steamy, but inside the air-conditioned Alamodome, 25,691 people—the largest crowd ever to watch a figure skating event anywhere in the world—saw a cool, calm, and collected Michelle put on a spectacular show filled with six flawless triple jumps. Michelle wowed the crowd, who responded with a rousing standing ovation, and the judges, who gave her the gold medal.

The crowd's reaction thrilled Michelle. "It was an incredible feeling to skate in front of that many people," Michelle said. "I went out there thinking, 'Oh my God,' when I heard all the people cheering for me."

As Michelle made her way up the ranks of senior skating, Frank Carroll wanted her to recognize the fact that she now faced greater competition than ever before, and she would have to work even harder. Michelle stepped up her training, trying all the while to balance her eighth-grade studies with her increased hours of skating.

Danny Kwan continued to drive the 200-mile round-trips to Lake Arrowhead to be with his daughters each day. The pressures were rising, and so were the costs—to nearly $60,000 per year. In order to maximize her earnings, Michelle signed with an agent, Shep Goldberg, in the fall of 1993.

Michelle was weak with the flu when she competed in Skate America in October 1993. In addition she was worried that a recent growth spurt—she was now 4' 11" and weighed 88 lbs.—would affect her jumps. Still, she believed that to be a champion one had to overcome all obstacles. So she went out and skated to a solid seventh-place finish.

Frank Carroll believed Michelle had tremendous potential at every level. "She's got the strongest total program of anyone in the Nationals. Nobody else is doing seven triple jumps," he declared.

In late 1993, Michelle confirmed Frank Carroll's ambitions for her as a junior skater. In her final performance as a junior, she won the 1994 Junior World Championships in Colorado Springs. She not only outskated the competition, but outjumped them as well. One of the skaters she bested was Germany's Tanya Szewczenko, who in the previous twelve months had beaten both reigning world champion Oksana Baiul and two-time Olympic medal winner Katerina Witt. Michelle's outstanding performance added to her growing reputation.

One skater who was impressed with Michelle's talents was Kristi Yamaguchi, the 1992 Olympic gold medal winner. "Michelle," Yamaguchi stated, "was much further advanced than I was at thirteen."

Michelle was quite proud and happy with her progress in 1993. "We had no expectations," she explained. "We just worked hard and all our dreams came true this year. It was a great, wonderful year."

1994 would bring bigger and better things for Michelle Kwan—a chance for a spot on the U.S. Olympic team and the possibility of an Olympic medal.

4

Olympic Dreams and Disappointments

As 1994 began, the prospect of two major skating events loomed: the Nationals in Detroit in January and the Winter Olympics in Lillehammer, Norway in February. The sports world was stunned in early January when an unknown assailant clubbed Nancy Kerrigan, the twenty-four-year-old reigning U.S. champion, on her knee after a pre-Nationals practice session. As Kerrigan sat on the sidelines nursing her bruised knee, Tonya Harding skated beautifully, landing five triple jumps and winning first-place votes from all nine judges to capture the national title. (Harding would later be disqualified when her then-husband's involvement in the attack on Kerrigan was brought to light.)

A year after defying her coach and taking the

senior test, Michelle continued to confirm that her instincts had been right. Now nearly five feet tall and weighing ninety pounds, Michelle looked like she belonged with the seniors both in terms of size *and* her skating. Her program at the 1994 Nationals was ambitious and demanding, and it included seven difficult triple jumps. She landed four flawlessly and fell once. But her program had been so technically challenging that the judges awarded her nine second-place votes and the silver medal.

For weeks Nancy Kerrigan's status as an Olympic team member remained uncertain. As a result of Michelle's second-place finish at the Nationals, she was named an alternate for Kerrigan. Michelle and her coach Frank Carroll were advised to begin a rigorous training program in anticipation of Michelle going to Norway.

"We're in limbo," Frank Carroll said. By late January, Kerrigan's knee still hadn't healed completely, so the U.S. Figure Skating Association sent Michelle a plane ticket for Norway. As an alternate, Michelle was not an actual member of the U.S. team. She was not allowed to live or skate with the rest of the Olympic team, and she and her coach would have to find accommodations on their own, miles away from the Olympic Village. "All we know," said Frank Carroll, "is we're going. Now at least we can get organized, do our laundry, and pack."

Just training for the Olympics gave Michelle a thrill. At age 13, she was poised to become the youngest U.S. figure skater ever to compete in a Winter Olympics. And because the public was riveted on the dramatic events surrounding Nancy Kerrigan, Michelle also found herself in the spotlight. Michelle was unfazed by all the attention. She simply said, "The only thing that has changed is that now I get to train in Norway, and that will be fun."

However, Michelle was in for a disappointment. During the final week in January, doctors examining Nancy Kerrigan found her able and eligible to compete in the Winter Games. The U.S. Figure Skating Association agreed and ruled that despite her absence at the Nationals, Kerrigan would skate in Norway.

Michelle's chances of making the Olympic team were growing slimmer by the day, but it didn't bother her too much. "I think it's fair," she said. "What I've gotten already is incredible."

Only two American skaters would be eligible to compete in the 1994 Winter Games. Despite the growing suspicion that Tonya Harding was somehow involved in the Kerrigan attack, her place on the Olympic skating team was still assured. However, Harding was not yet totally in the clear so Michelle still had a slim hope of skating on the team. "If somebody can't go, I'll be prepared," she said.

Michelle's coach tried to keep her focused on her skating and her training, instead of the skating soap opera that was unfolding. "This other stuff, she doesn't understand it. Her job is to skate," Frank Carroll explained.

Michelle was still listed as an alternate, but any hopes she had of actually skating in Norway were dashed when the final decision was made to allow Tonya Harding to compete. Michelle would have to content herself with the possibility of making it to the next Olympics—the 1998 Games in Nagano, Japan—instead.

Because of the events of January, Nancy Kerrigan decided not to compete in the 1994 Worlds in Chiba, Japan in March 1994. Michelle was selected to take her place. Again this was based on her second-place showing at the Nationals. At age 13, Michelle was the youngest person to represent the United States in the Worlds. "The little girl," as one writer described Michelle, appeared somewhat awestruck as she took to the ice Friday evening, March 25. Despite her high hopes, Michelle was in for another disappointment.

During her short program, she fell on a triple lutz and missed a critical combination jump. Michelle had moments where she looked utterly beautiful on the ice, but when the first round was over, she was in eleventh place. Still, Michelle was determined to put her performance behind her. "What's done is done," she said. "You can't rewind or record over it."

Michelle seemed more sure of herself in the four-minute free skate program. She landed six of seven triple jumps cleanly and rose to eighth place in the final standings. For a thirteen-year-old, it was an impressive achievement.

"I'm really happy it ended this way," Michelle

said, and with good reason. Had she finished out of the top ten, she would not have been eligible to go to the 1995 Worlds in Birmingham, England the following year.

Michelle had also learned an important lesson. "Whether you're nervous or not, you still have to go out there and try your best. You have to have energy out there," she told a reporter.

The following month Michelle again landed six of seven triple jumps and skated to a second-place finish in the Hershey's Kisses Pro-Am tournament. Judges recognized the technical merit of her program, giving her eight 5.9s. However, they gave her lower scores for her artistic merit, and Michelle ended up being outskated by Caryn Kadavy, a more experienced skater and former Olympian who had turned professional. Michelle did finish ahead of three-time national champion Rosalynn Summers to capture the $30,000 second-prize money. Michelle was happiest, though, about the six first-place votes she received from the nine judges.

If there was a flaw in Michelle's skating, it was that her style lacked maturity, it was said. Observers pointed out that at age 13, projecting a mature artistic image was not something Michelle was capable of. Michelle was undisturbed by the comments.

"I felt good, but I could have done better," she remarked. "It just didn't happen." Michelle was proud to have skated with such world-class skaters as Kadavy and Summers. "It was really exciting to be out there skating with the people I saw in the

Olympics," Michelle said. "It's just a great experience being here. But it's hard. The competition is hard."

The winner, Caryn Kadavy, was definitely impressed by Michelle's performance. "She is our future," Kadavy told reporters. "She's very mature for her age, but she still has time to mature more. That will come with age."

Michelle had now been skating almost nonstop since the previous summer and her coach was concerned that she was getting tired. Michelle understood her coach's concern, but she believed she could keep up with the accelerated pace of international competition.

In August 1994, a month after her fourteenth birthday, Michelle traveled to Russia for the Goodwill Games. In her short program, she struggled and finished sixth out of eight skaters. But the next day she returned to the ice for her free skate, and she regained her poise and form. She landed seven triple jumps and was one of only three women who did not fall. In the second half of the competition, she outskated Surya Bonaly, a high-flying French skater who had won four European championships.

Michelle's style was maturing, and she seemed more aware of the crowd. Michelle had been studying Olympic gold medalist Oksana Baiul, and she'd noticed how the Russian skater played to the audience. Michelle concluded her own free skate program with a radiant smile, blowing kisses to the crowd. The fans were equally enthusiastic and gave her a rousing ovation in return. Michelle was ecstatic as she left the ice. Danny rushed up to her, and father and daughter exchanged an exuberant high five. Moments later, Michelle's scores were announced. They put her in first in the free skate.

Michelle's outstanding free skate performance put her in second place overall, right behind Surya Bonaly. "This is a new notch in her belt," said Frank Carroll, "beating Surya in the free."

Michelle arrived in Pittsburgh in late October 1994 to compete in the Skate America tournament, where she improved on her previous year's seventh-place finish by placing second. After picking up a check for $7,500 in prize money, Michelle packed up her skating costume and traded it in for a Halloween costume. Dressed as Fred Flintstone, Michelle and her sister Karen, wearing a Pebbles costume, walked around their hometown of Torrance, trick-or-treating like regular teenagers. For one evening, at least, the pressure was off, as Michelle strolled around her hometown unrecognized.

Michelle's family was determined to protect Michelle from the stresses of skating and to make sure her childhood remained fun. "You have to figure out what you want, a gold medal or to have fun," Danny Kwan said, summing up the family's philosophy. "We want to have fun."

Always a tight-knit family, the Kwans were now getting to spend more time together. Estella had moved into her daughters' tiny cabin, and while Danny continued his shuttle back and forth between Lake Arrowhead and the family restaurant, he too was able to be with his daughters more. Both Michelle and Karen were grateful for the increased time they got to spend with their parents.

5

Rising up the Ranks

During Thanksgiving 1994, Tara and her parents traveled to Budapest, Hungary for the 1995 World Junior championship. It was fun for Tara to be in a foreign city, but she was also quite focused on skating well. Carolyne Kruse, a skating official who stayed in the same hotel as Tara, remembers that Tara was not only organized, but also a natural team leader.

"One night she comes walking down the hallway of the hotel with her long nightgown on and these huge rollers in her hair," Kruse recalled. "Mind you, she's only twelve years old, and she says, 'Now you guys go to bed and be quiet. I've got an early practice.' And all the kids were real quiet and went to bed."

Competing at the championship, Tara impressed the international audience with her jumps and lively presentation. She finished fourth, ahead of many skaters who were older and more experienced.

"Fourth in the world," Jack said to Pat. "Do you know how good that is?"

"I know," Pat said, with some apprehension.

Pat could see that the pressure on Tara was building, and she worried what it might do to her daughter. However, Tara seemed immune to it.

Meanwhile, there was financial pressure, too. The quest for skating success was growing more expensive each year. The Lipinskis were already spending more than $50,000 a year for coaching, ice time, skates, and costumes (some of which cost up to $1,000).

The 1995 National Junior championship was set for the beginning of February 1995, and Tara trained hard for them. She skated five 40-minute sessions every day but Saturday. Schoolwork was crammed into two-hour-a-day tutoring sessions.

Tara was determined to add an ambitious and difficult triple flip to her program, but neither her parents nor her coach were persuaded that she should risk the move in the upcoming championship. At the Gold Arena at the University of Delaware, Tara practiced the jump endlessly. What set Tara apart was her ability to spin so quickly while in the air. She did not jump as high as some skaters, but she managed to whirl fast enough to complete her revolutions anyway.

"She doesn't want one jump perfect," her coach told a visitor. "She wants everything perfect."

Finally Tara was ready to prove she could do it. As her parents and coach watched anxiously from the side of the rink, Tara glided backwards along a smooth arc across the ice. She dug her toe picks into the ice, then flew into the air. She made three tight revolutions in mid-air and landed cleanly, finishing with her arms extended above her head. Tara smiled at her parents and coach. She had convinced them, and she knew it.

Expectations for Tara were running high at the National Juniors scheduled to take place in Providence, Rhode Island. Recently Claire Ferguson, the president of the U.S. Figure Skating Association, had been quoted in the *Providence Journal* as saying, "Tara Lipinski is going to be something else." She included tiny Tara in the ranks of unknown skaters who'd gone on to greatness, skaters like Dorothy Hamill, Todd Eldredge, and Michelle Kwan.

The media loved the 4' 5", 69-pound Tara. And Tara appeared totally at ease surrounded by reporters, photographers, and TV camera crews at a precompetition press conference. "I love the cameras," Tara said with genuine pleasure.

Tara was asked what her goals were. She answered, "To win the Olympics."

"Which one?" a reporter asked, wondering if Tara had the 1998 or the 2001 Games in mind.

"Whatever one," Tara said without hesitation.

Jere Longman, a *New York Times* reporter, declared that "there was not a younger, more talented or confident skater at the junior level." She added that Tara's "self-assurance, poise, and maturity translate to grace and power on the ice unmatched by any American female skater her age, and few of any age."

By the time Tara was ready to skate at the National Juniors, Pat and Jack had grown more than a little nervous about all the hype, but they tried not to show it. "You'll do fine," Pat told her daughter.

"I know," an ever-confident Tara replied as she gave her mother a reassuring kiss on the cheek.

Tara was scheduled to skate first in the short program. That was considered a disadvantage. Sometimes judges gave the first skater lower scores in order to leave room for better scores as the later skaters performed.

There were barely 1,600 people in the cavernous Providence Civic Center when Tara emerged on the ice wearing a black velvet dress and black gloves. She easily completed her triple loop–double loop combination, double axel, and a double flip, and she avoided making any major mistakes. When she came off the ice, Tara was happy to see that her technical scores were good but was disappointed to see that only two of nine judges gave her top marks for artistic presentation. The judges seemed to be saying that, technically, Tara was solid, but that her style and presentation werc just not as well developed.

Tara, however, had the lead and kept it until

Sydne Vogel, a promising fifteen-year-old from Anchorage, Alaska, came out for her short program. To some observers, Vogel skated with more maturity and style than Tara, and the judges must have agreed. When Vogel's scores were announced, she had bumped Tara into second place.

Still, both Tara and her coach were happy with Tara's showing. "That was the best I've ever seen her skate," her coach Jeff DiGregorio declared.

Tara was more than happy with her performance. "The more big competitions I do," she declared, "the better I feel about myself. I love skating and I like all of this," she said, gesturing towards the crush of reporters and photographers.

Twice as many people showed up for the long program as for the short. Tara hoped to come from behind and win with a program featuring six triple jumps, including a rarely performed triple flip that she had been practicing for months. Tara had topped Vogel in the National Novice Championship the year before—placing second to Vogel's fifth—and she hoped to outskate the Alaskan again.

In the free skate, Vogel skated ahead of Tara. Starting strong with a smooth triple lutz, Vogel continued to perform flawlessly. But she seemed to be getting tired, and when the Alaskan teen tried a double axel, she landed awkwardly and fell to the ice. Her final move was supposed to be a triple toe, but Vogel stumbled and managed only a single. Despite her fall, the judges gave Vogel solid technical scores because of her successful triple lutz. And again her artistry marks were above average. Six judges gave Vogel first-place votes.

Tara was the last skater to compete. Skating to the music of *Samson and Delilah,* she looked nervous at first and seemed a little uncertain on her triple jump. Then Tara took control and skated what many considered to be a perfect long program. She landed the rest of her triple jumps smoothly, including her much-practiced triple flip.

Tara was overjoyed when she came off the ice. She and her coach hugged, then looked up, anxiously awaiting the scores. Tara's technical marks were good enough to put her in a tie with Vogel, but when her artistic marks were announced, Tara and her coach were disappointed to see mostly 5.0s and 5.1s. The tie was broken and Vogel had won. As she walked backstage, Tara struggled to hold back her tears. Later, Tara climbed into the stands to sit with her parents and she began to cry.

Only two judges had given Tara first-place votes. More than a few people suspected the lower marks were a result of Tara's size. Tara had to settle for the silver medal and she was not happy. "I'll beat her next year," Tara vowed.

"She's fighting mad," Ron Ludington, director of the University of Delaware's skating program, said after talking with Tara. "She'd love to do it all over again, I'm sure. I think her size works against her. She's a little girl and that comes across."

Her coach Jeff DiGregorio tried to remain positive. "I was very proud of the way Tara skated. She was the best in my eyes. I would have put her first. This keeps her hungry. I think there's a national title in Tara's future," he predicted. Later, DiGregorio would come to believe Tara's defeat had been a blessing in disguise, for it would drive her to work even harder.

Tara's size was also generating some controversy. Some said she was too small and her body wasn't strong enough to do triple jumps. But the Lipinskis and Jeff DiGregorio had consulted with doctors who said she had both the muscles and bone structure to withstand the physical stress. Tara, the doctors said, would probably not grow taller than 5' 1". Still, there were skeptics who said that once Tara began to grow, she would not be able to complete a triple jump without some difficulty. "It won't last," one well-known coach was heard to say.

Other writers took potshots at Tara for her youth. One reporter from the *Providence Journal* questioned whether Tara was being forced at an early age to compete at a level for which she was not prepared. Was Tara being pushed too hard? he asked. "How does a twelve-year-old know exactly what she wants to do?"

"Nobody has to push Tara," Jeff DiGregorio responded. "Tara sets her own agenda. She loves to train and she loves to skate. And she pushes herself."

Tara *was* pushing herself, and she had a new goal—to compete in the 1996 Nationals. But this time she wanted to compete as a senior, not a junior. Again, there were doubters. "She doesn't have the skating ability to win the juniors," suggested Bonnie McLauthlin, a veteran judge who'd watched the recent junior championship.

Despite questions about her youth, size, and ambition, Tara was basking in the glow of skating success. A few weeks after the Nationals, Tara was profiled on the TV program *Prime Time Live*. In a *Sports Illustrated* article on the 1995 Junior Nationals, there was a photo of just one junior skater. It was Tara.

Tara's career was gaining more and more momentum. Not long after her thirteenth birthday, Tara got an agent, Mike Burg, a former television executive and promoter from North Carolina. Burg had convinced the Lipinskis that he could help Tara not only rise up the ranks but also earn up to as much as $100,000 over the next few years by appearing in various competitions and exhibitions. The money would certainly come in handy. The Lipinskis were now spending nearly $60,000 a year to keep Tara in training.

Tara was convinced she was ready to make the jump to the senior level. So was her coach, who was certain Tara had what it took to be a champion, even on the senior level. Others, including some judges, skating officials, and friends of the Lipinskis, thought Tara should remain a junior for another year. Her jumps needed work, they said.

What they didn't understand, DiGregorio told everyone, was that "Tara wants to do it. She wants the next challenge." For Tara, making it to the 1996

Senior National championship was the next step up the ladder.

As 1995 drew to a close, the Lipinskis had plenty to be happy about. They were delighted with Tara's second-place finish in the National Juniors, but it had become clear that if Tara were to compete as a senior skater, she would require a new approach, new moves, and a new coach with a proven track record for coaching young skaters to national titles.

Pat and Tara interviewed several coaches, including Kathy Casey and Carlo Fassi, who guided world champion skaters such as Peggy Fleming. They met with Richard Callaghan, who'd coached champions like Todd Eldredge and Nicole Bobek. Tara and Pat liked Callaghan and his approach, and his training program seemed just right for Tara. So they signed up with him, moved to Bloomfield Hills, Michigan, and joined the Detroit Skating Club.

Eldredge, another member of the Detroit Skating Club who would go on to win the national title in 1995 and the Worlds in 1996, was immediately impressed by Tara's self-confidence and outgoing manner. "Most kids, you'd think if they were around their idols or whatever, they'd be a little shy. But she wasn't that way. She'd come up and ask anything," he related.

Tara's signing with Callaghan and her moving once again reignited the controversy about whether young athletes like Tara were being pushed too hard to achieve success. The controversy eventually grew to include other young athletes such as gymnasts.

But Tara was nearly always the example to which people pointed in the debate.

Tara was quick to point out that she loved what she was doing, and that no one had pushed her into it.

"Listen," her new coach told reporters, "she loves to skate. Period. And she loves to win."

6

Michelle's Makeover

While Tara's youth was creating controversy, Michelle Kwan was being hailed more and more for her maturity and style. Already considered a strong jumper, she was now being recognized for her growing artistry and expressiveness on the ice. Long-time observers of the skating scene compared her to greats like Peggy Fleming and Kristi Yamaguchi, saying she had the kind of discipline and dedication that all great champions must have.

The weather was bitterly cold in Providence, Rhode Island when the 1995 National Seniors got underway in early February. Michelle, at fourteen, had the potential to become the youngest U.S. champ ever. She had skated well throughout the previous fall, topping her chief rival, seventeen-year-old Nicole Bobek, in three events. Bobek, a confident, creative, and showy skater, had won a bronze medal at the previous year's Nationals with her jumps, so she was a strong candidate for gold at the Nationals. So was the veteran Tonia Kwiatkowski. But many were convinced that Michelle's time had come.

"I think it's great to be called the next national champion," Michelle admitted. "I've worked a lot on my style and artistry. But I don't think there's any pressure. We're still the underdog. I'm thinking this is just a normal competition and not worrying about any results."

If Michelle wasn't feeling the pressure, Nicole Bobek was, and she didn't have to look far to see the reasons why.

"There's Kwan and a whole bunch of little kids behind me," Nicole Bobek said. "I feel old. I know I can't afford to make mistakes, because these girls are right behind me." Bobek could be a sensational skater when she was in shape, and now, having lost ten pounds and having practiced hard in recent months, she was in top form.

Michelle skated well in her short program but stumbled on her triple lutz–double toe combination. The mistakes were enough to put her in third place behind Kwiatkowski and Bobek.

The weather turned warmer by Saturday, the day of the free skate, and the competition grew hotter, too. Tonia Kwiatkowski fell on one of her jumps and had a bad landing on another. That knocked her out of the top three.

Nicole Bobek knew she had to skate aggressively to take the lead, and she psyched herself up as she walked towards the ice. "Attack," she told herself. Bobek began with an elegant spiral that won admiring oohs and ahhs from the crowd. Although she faltered a bit on a triple toe loop, she managed to avoid serious mistakes for the rest of her program. When she skated off the ice, she was greeted by solid scores ranging from 5.7s to 5.9s. Bobek was in first.

Michelle was the final skater in the competition. Wearing a bubblegum-pink, sequined costume, Michelle planned a stylish and challenging program loaded with triple jumps. Her opening was solid, and midway through the program she performed a picture-perfect triple lutz. With just thirty seconds left, Michelle began to pick up speed. She would need the momentum to get enough height to do her final triple lutz.

On the sidelines, Frank Carroll sensed something was wrong. Michelle was not skating fast enough. Moments later, Michelle leaped into the air, whirled around, then fell to the ice as she landed. She quickly got to her feet, but there was no doubt: the mistake would hurt her scores. Michelle's marks weren't bad—5.6s and several 5.9s. However, only one judge gave her a first-place vote. Eight judges awarded Bobek the top spot, and she was crowned the new national champion. Michelle's family consoled themselves with a second-place finish, but it was a disappointment for Michelle. The speculation was that several judges considered Nicole a more mature and poised performer than the youthful Michelle.

"We knew it would be a tough battle," Frank Carroll said later. Michelle, he added, "would live to skate another day."

Thanks to their showings at the 1995 Nationals, both Michelle and Nicole Bobek were signed up for an ice show that was scheduled to travel all over the world for most of the spring and summer. Michelle skated in sixty-five shows, and her skating was admired not only by the spectators but also by her fellow skaters, including Brian Boitano, the one who had inspired Michelle years earlier, and future world champion Elvis Stojko. When Michelle wasn't practicing her triple axel with Boitano and Stojko she could be found doing her homework in her hotel room. By the end of the tour, it was clear that skating with champions had sharpened Michelle's skills. "Great skating breeds great skating," Frank Carroll noted.

Great skating could also make great money. As a result of her rise in the ranks and the tours and exhibitions, Michelle was now earning $750,000 a year.

Michelle acknowledged that she still had a lot to learn in terms of feeling and interpreting the music and expressing herself more creatively on the ice. Two years later Michelle would look back and say, "At fourteen, I didn't know much of anything. I never really developed my skating. I just jumped and jumped and jumped some more. It wasn't really artistic. I kind of smiled once in a while and laughed it off. But you want to feel what's inside and portray it and express it to the audience."

As another result of their showing at the Nationals, both Bobek and Michelle earned invitations to compete at the 1995 Worlds, scheduled to take place in Birmingham, England.

In mid-March, Michelle and her father flew to London, where they spent several days sightseeing. They visited Big Ben and Buckingham Palace, then rode the train north to the industrial city of Birmingham.

Prior to the Worlds, Michelle and her coach had rethought her routine, shuffling the order of her most difficult moves in order to conserve her strength. Her program was still among the most demanding of all the women skaters who had come to Birmingham.

"I was ready for something new and it was the perfect time," Michelle would say later.

Carroll also offered some simple advice to Michelle. "Smile more," he suggested.

The changes in her routine must have helped because Michelle skated a flawless short program. The audience cheered loudly, and when she finished, a shower of flowers and stuffed animals rained down on the ice. However, when Michelle's scores were announced, the applause turned to boos. The judges had scored Michelle lower than the European champion Surya Bonaly of France, who to most observers had skated a sloppy program. A French coach, however, sniffed that Michelle's skating was clearly "junior skating," not world-class like Bonaly's.

Nicole Bobek won the short program, followed closely by China's Chen Lu. Michelle finished in fifth.

At a press conference later, Michelle was philosophical. "I went for everything I've got and just gave it my best shot," she said with quiet dignity. "It turned out great. I had nothing to lose. You might be the best in your heart, but not in other people's sight."

There was still the long program, which counted for two-thirds of the final score. In front of an audience of 7,000, Nicole Bobek performed well at first, but then fell on two triple jumps. When she left the ice, she was in tears. She knew she had lost her lead. Chen Lu skated superbly to take the lead, and Surya Bonaly's six triples landed her in second place.

Michelle skated last. She seemed calm and confident as she circled the rink. After she successfully landed her triple lutz—the same jump that had cost her so much at the 1995 Nationals—she threw in an unplanned double toe loop. When she landed it perfectly, she and Carroll broke into simultaneous smiles. Only seconds remained as Michelle sailed through her final triple jump, and like all the six previous ones, she landed it smoothly.

The music stopped and Michelle bowed at center

ice. The crowd rose as one and tumultuous applause filled the arena. Michelle was overcome by emotion. She raised her hands to her face as tears trickled down her cheeks. It was as if a dam had broken and the pressure, for just one moment, had eased into the joy of athletic accomplishment. Even her seasoned coach found himself with tears in his eyes as he planted a kiss on top of Michelle's head.

Michelle's third-place performance in the free skate raised her to fourth place overall. But many observers questioned why she had not won a medal. Both her short program and long program were as challenging and difficult as anyone else's, and she had received two first-place votes. However, Chen Lu had won three first-place votes, and when the final scores were tallied, the Chinese skater was the new world champion. Surya Bonaly claimed the silver medal and Nicole Bobek the bronze. Michelle had finished just tenths of a point out of medal contention.

Despite her showing, Michelle was happy with her performance, and she took comfort in the fact that the crowd had given her such strong support. She was the only woman skater to win a standing ovation.

"It was just so overwhelming—all the American flags waving and everyone standing," Michelle said.

Frank Carroll was disappointed, not in Michelle, but in the judges. He believed that Michelle's youthful appearance had worked against her, that her pony tail and lack of makeup had led judges to think she was more a child than a woman, and because of that they had unconsciously graded her lower. "The judges are looking at her and they're saying, 'She's 14. Is she ready to be the best free skater in the world?' I think that had a lot to do with it—her age," Carroll stated.

A reporter from the *Los Angeles Times* who had covered Michelle's career from its earliest days declared that "the only thing Michelle Kwan did wrong was to be fourteen years old."

Danny Kwan was not worried. "This is not about winning or losing," he said. "Michelle skated better than she ever has before. The scoring depends a lot on artistry and Michelle doesn't have the body of a grown woman yet. She's still a young girl. But she's fourth in the world and she's fourteen years old. I'm satisfied. There's still a long time to come."

And there was still a lot of work to do, Michelle knew. "I have to work on my triple-triple. My performance has to flow more. And my spins have to be faster," she emphasized.

Carroll predicted other changes in the coming season. He had already talked to Michelle about wearing her hair up in a more mature way and wearing costumes with bolder colors and more sophisticated styles. In addition, he wanted Michelle to wear more makeup to make her look older and more elegant.

Michelle and Carroll did not have to wait long for proof that she could skate and win against the world's best. Shortly after the 1995 Worlds, Michelle won her first international competition as a senior, taking first in the Hershey's Kisses International Figure Skating Challenge. Not only did she beat U.S. champion Nicole Bobek, but she also beat Surya Bonaly, the French skater who had won the silver medal at the Worlds just weeks earlier.

Michelle's fall season was filled with successes. She took first in both the Skate America and Skate Canada competitions. Later she was invited to dedicate an outdoor skating rink at Disneyland, not far from her home. She skated to music from the film *Pocahantas* and was showered by fans with flowers and stuffed animals. She gave impromptu skating lessons, then donated the toys to a group of young patients at Children's Hospital in Los Angeles.

With all the attention she was receiving, the rest of the family was concerned about Michelle becoming overconfident. "Don't start thinking you're special," Danny kept saying to her. But there was no doubt— Michelle was special, and as the coming season approached, many predicted that Michelle would demonstrate just what a great skater she was.

The 1995–96 season began in the fall, and Michelle dominated the field with a series of polished performances. Many fans noted that Michelle's style had grown more artistic, and her movements, hand gestures, and facial expressions more elegant. The girl who said earlier that "I didn't even know what artistic was," had suddenly bloomed into a supremely expressive skater.

Her look had changed, too. Barely a year before,

she had worn only the slightest trace of lipstick. Now, her eyebrows had been shaped and her make-up was sophisticated and stylish. The ponytail was replaced by a braided, tightly sewn bun. Gone were the pink bubblegum—colored costumes she had worn earlier, and in their place were more elegant skating dresses.

Michelle's appearance was so different that when she and Carroll were seen together, some wondered who was the new young woman Carroll was coaching.

It had not been easy for Carroll to convince Michelle's parents that the makeover was the right move. Being a traditional Chinese-American family, Danny and Estella did not believe a young girl should wear makeup. But Carroll had convinced them that one reason the judges had ranked Michelle fourth in the 1995 Worlds was that she appeared to be a little girl. With her new look, Carroll predicted, Michelle would be seen as a young woman, and that would help her scores.

Positive results were not long in coming. First Michelle traveled to Detroit, where she easily won the Skate America competition. Just over the border a few weeks later, she took the gold medal in the Skate Canada competition. Then she hopped on a plane to Frankfurt, Germany, where she again out-performed the competition, including 1995 national champion Nicole Bobek, taking first in the Nations Cup competition. With the 1996 U.S. Nationals and Worlds coming up, Michelle Kwan was skating in peak form, and she was considered a favorite for first in both events.

The 1996 U.S. Nationals were set for late January in San Jose, California. Michelle was optimistic about her chances and she told reporters that in addition to her looks, her skating style had also grown more refined.

"I made a lot of changes this year and I'm very comfortable with them," she said. "I've always had an image in my mind. It has to come from inside. You have to feel the music, the emotion, from inside, not just the outside look."

Skating in front of a crowd packed with her fans, Michelle performed what *Sports Illustrated* called "a brilliant and mature [short] program." It featured seven triple jumps and a spectacular triple toe–triple loop combination. Her performance was smooth and flowing, and the maturity Carroll hoped Michelle would show the world—and the judges— was clearly evident, and her solid short program scores reflected it. Michelle's elegant long program sealed her victory over second-place finisher Tonia Kwiatkowski. Right behind them in third place was thirteen-year-old Tara Lipinski.

Now 5' 2" and weighing 98 pounds, fifteen-year-old Michelle Kwan was crowned as the youngest ladies U.S. champion since Peggy Fleming took the title in 1964.

"Certainly I skated my best," was all Michelle could say. No one who watched her in San Jose would disagree.

At thirteen, Tara had still been eligible to compete in the 1996 World Junior championship, where she had been considered the favorite for the gold medal. Perhaps distracted by the prospect of skating in the upcoming National Senior championship, Tara finished a disappointing fifth in the National Juniors. But at the National Seniors in San Jose, California, Tara skated in top form, landing five triple jumps and a triple lutz–double toe combination that won her the bronze medal. She was thrilled to have placed in the top three. "It's so weird I'm right behind Michelle and Tonia. When I was standing on the podium, I was like, 'Oh my gosh. I've watched them on TV!'"

It would be the first of many times that Michelle Kwan and Tara Lipinski would share a winners' podium.

On the Worlds Stage

As a result of Tara's third-place finish in the 1996 Nationals, she was selected to join Michelle and Tonia Kwiatkowski on the 1996 Worlds team. Because of an injury, Nicole Bobek, the 1995 national champ, had had to withdraw from the 1996 Nationals. That led to the decision to give Tara the third spot on the Worlds team. The move caused some complaints because Bobek had won the bronze at the Worlds the year before. Tara took it all in stride.

"I'm friends with Nicole so either way was okay with me," she said. "I was just happy I skated well [at the Nationals]."

In March Tara joined her teammates in Edmonton, Alberta, the site of the 1996 Worlds. Michelle

72

arrived as the heavy favorite. She had won five of her last six international events. The one event she hadn't won was at the Centennial On Ice competition in Russia when she had been ill but still finished third.

In addition to her vigorous training, Michelle had continued to refine her look. She had spent the last year studying the styles of previous women champions, and the sophisticated, grown-up look she introduced at the 1996 Nationals now seemed natural and fitting.

"I learned from the Olympic champions," Michelle revealed. "I looked in the mirror and examined how they did their makeup. I learned from the best." Michelle was confident that this time she would win a medal in the Worlds, unlike the year before.

Michelle's skating had continued to mature too, as she demonstrated in the short program. Combining her already-impressive jumping abilities with a new expressiveness and artistry, she performed a flawless triple lutz–double toe combination, then landed an exquisite double axel. She seemed to float, feather-like, as she whirled through a series of spirals and spins that earned her seven 5.9s and a standing ovation. She gained nine first-place votes, giving her a solid lead over defending world champion Chen Lu and Russian teenager Irina Slutskaya.

Sometimes, in a pressure-filled event like the Worlds, a skater will leave her best performance on the practice ice. That's exactly what happened to

Tara, the youngest skater in Edmonton. After a perfect practice, Tara was set to skate her short program right after one of her idols, Japan's Midori Ito. Ito, a superb, strong jumper, was sick, but she competed anyway. She took a bad fall, which knocked her out of contention for a medal.

Perhaps sensing an opportunity to outskate one of her heroes, Tara tried too hard and had a disastrous short program. Her landing on her triple lutz was a difficult one, and then she fell on a double loop, a jump that usually came easy for her. Hoping to recover, Tara tried a triple loop but fell again. As she scrambled to her feet, she cast a worried look to her coach on the sidelines. Callaghan offered a nod of encouragement to Tara as she wrapped up her program. The judges weren't as sympathetic. Their scores dropped Tara to twenty-third place. Had she finished one place lower she would have been eliminated.

The doubters who said she wasn't ready to compete as a senior in the Worlds were ready with a chorus of smug "I told you so's."

Her coach thought that Tara had been affected by Midori Ito's less-than-perfect performance. "Tara thought she had a chance to beat this great star and she tried too hard," he suggested.

Whatever the reason, Tara was devastated. "I was so low, so down that first day," she later recalled. Still, she was determined to do better in the long program and show everyone that she truly deserved to be at the Worlds.

Michelle had won the short program decisively. She was elated not only by her first-place finish but also by the audience's reaction.

"When you're dreaming of doing a clean program, you don't dream about the audience clapping and getting a standing ovation. This afternoon, it was incredible, just the feeling once I stepped on the ice, I knew I was at the world championship, and the audience was magnificent. They were all rooting for me. I can't explain the feeling that a skater gets when they're out there."

"Michelle had a vision of how to go about this," her coach noted. "Her first Worlds, she was in awe. She was flattered to be among the other skaters. The last couple of years, she had a plan of how to be one of the best. It included her personal look, moves, and music, to do something extraordinary instead of ordinary."

Saturday's long program was shaping up to be an exciting climax to the 1996 Worlds. The night before, Michelle ran through her long program in her head, visualizing a clean, error-free performance. The challenge, she knew, would be to do it on the ice.

Defending world champion Chen Lu went onto the ice first. Her skating was magnificent, and she showed the same grace and style that had won her the 1995 Worlds. While the Chinese champion performed, Michelle and Frank Carroll sought a quiet place where they could talk. They slipped into a closet-sized room, hoping for a few calming moments. Instead they heard the crowd chanting "Six, Six, Six," urging the judges to award Chen perfect marks. Then they heard the judges announce that Chen's scores did indeed include two perfect 6's for artistic merit. Michelle's heart sank and she had a sudden attack of nerves. "Oh my God," she said to Carroll, "I'll have to do a *quadruple* toe loop to win."

Michelle knew she would need to give the performance of a lifetime to top Chen. At first she had doubts. "Then," she recalled, "I got myself down to earth and said, 'Just go for it. Go for everything, why not?'"

Carroll calmed her, too, saying, "Those were fabulous marks, but the judges left room for you to win. You've got to believe in yourself, that you can do it. You're one of the best skaters in the world."

"I know," Michelle replied softly. Carroll could see the determination in Michelle's eyes. At that moment, he would later say, "I knew right then she was going to win."

Twenty minutes later, Michelle stepped onto the ice, looking like an Arabian princess in a two-piece blue silk costume. Before she began skating, she rubbed her hands on the ice and brought them to her neck. As she felt the cold on her skin, she felt refreshed and alert.

Skating to "Dance of the Veils," Michelle gave a mesmerizing performance. She moved with the grace of a ballet dancer, using her arm movements, hand gestures, and facial expressions to add color and depth to her routine. She was also steady as a rock on her jumps. Michelle landed six triple jumps cleanly, then in the final seconds of the program, nearing exhaustion, she launched herself into an unplanned triple toe loop. As she landed, the crowd began chanting "Six! Six! Six!" That final jump gave her one more triple than Chen Lu and a slight edge over the Chinese champion. The crowd rose in a standing ovation. Michelle was so overcome with emotion that tears began streaming down her cheeks.

"The emotions took over when I realized this was the world championship and I had just skated the best I ever had in my life," she said. "I knew I had done it at the right moment."

The judges agreed. Two gave her 6.0s and seven gave her 5.9s. Six of the judges had her in first place, and Michelle took the lead.

Tara fingered the good-luck charm she wore around her neck as she waited for her turn to skate her long program. The necklace contained tiny gold skates, hearts, and a "thumbs up" emblem. It must have helped, because Tara regained her form in the long program. As the music from the soundtrack of *Speed* resounded through the arena, Tara nailed seven triple jumps without so much as a stumble to finish eleventh in the free skate. Her performance pulled her up to fifteenth place overall, a solid finish for a thirteen-year-old. Tara knew she had skated well when the audience gave her a standing ovation.

"This was really great," she said after she finished.

"I felt great when I started to land everything. I wanted to stay out there forever. I didn't want to get off the ice."

No one topped Michelle, however, and she was named the new world champion. At fifteen, Michelle's victory had made her the third-youngest ladies' world champion ever after Sonja Henie, who captured her first world title in 1927, and Oksana Baiul, who did it in 1993. Michelle was overwhelmed by her feelings, and as she stood on the podium wearing her gold medal, she began to cry. It had been an extraordinary season for her and the world title was the crowning achievement.

Moments later, Michelle looked a bit bewildered when she bounded into the postvictory press conference. She still had her makeup on and her hair was still in a bun. On her back she wore a teddy bear knapsack. It hadn't quite sunk in yet that she had won.

"I'm fifteen years old and I'm the world champion," she exclaimed, then cupped her hands over her mouth in disbelief. "I can't believe it fits me—world champion!"

When she regained her composure, she said that winning the Worlds "has been a dream of mine, something I thought about doing since I started out. It's the highlight of my life." Shaking her head, she confessed, "I can't really get it in my brain that I did it."

The moment was a great one for her coach, too. Carroll had taken a lot of criticism for Michelle's makeover, but now he felt totally vindicated. Michelle, he said, had it all—athletic skill and artistic style. Recalling the "junior skating" comments made about Michelle at the previous Worlds, he added, "She's not a kid anymore. She's definitely a young lady."

To win a world title, he told a crowd of reporters, "You've got to be very athletic, but if you don't have the look, the choreography, the music, it's impossible to be a world champion."

Michelle was still wearing her gold medal when she went to bed that night, and she kept it on all night. When she woke up, she had a realization. "It was like, I won, now get on with life." Michelle had incorporated a new maturity in her skating. Now, she was living it.

Michelle's earnings soared. Thanks to her world title, she would earn more than $1 million from prize money and special appearances in 1996. During the summer, Michelle joined a skating tour that crisscrossed the country. The tour was well attended all across the country, and Michelle was one of the biggest draws.

The tour was fun, but also a bit grueling. One day, after a particularly tiring performance, Michelle climbed on the bus, trying to avoid the fans clamoring for autographs. Michelle was weary, but Danny insisted she go out and sign autographs.

"All the things you have come from them," he told Michelle. "Learn to give back." He also reminded her to learn to be satisfied with her achievements.

No matter what happened in the future, he said proudly, she was already a champion.

Before the year had ended, Michelle had led a U.S. sweep of the Skate America competition against a top-ranked international field of skaters in Springfield, Massachusetts. She unveiled a new free skate program and new music, "The Love Story Behind the Taj Mahal," from *Lawrence of Arabia*. Her performance dazzled the crowd and the judges, who gave her nine first-place votes to top her teammates Tonia Kwiatkowski and Sydne Vogel.

During the summer of 1996 Tara took time out to watch the Olympic Games in Atlanta. She was thrilled by the gold-medal performance by the U.S. women's gymnastic team. Later that summer, Tara met one of those gymnasts, Dominique Moceanu. The two have been good friends ever since.

The fall of 1996 brought a new busy skating season. Tara introduced a new program and won second place at the Skate Canada competition in Kitchener, Ontario. Michelle and Tara both traveled to Paris to participate in the Trophy Lalique competition. Michelle, skating in peak form, won the event, while Tara claimed the bronze medal.

The trip was even more rewarding for Tara because Jack had joined Tara and Pat in Paris, and the family got to enjoy a brief vacation sightseeing in the French capital. A few days later, when it became apparent that the still-injured Nicole Bobek would not make the Nations Cup competition in Gelsenkirchen, Tara was invited to take her place. She won the silver medal, and was outdone only by Russian Irina Slutskaya, the third-place finisher in the previous world championship. Tara's solid showing earned her the chance to compete at the Champions Series Finals, scheduled for late February 1997 in Canada.

Tara's schedule was dizzying. "To go from the U.S. to Canada, to Paris to Germany in three weeks, and then be asked to compete against the world's best, was a little overwhelming," she said. "But once I was on the ice, I knew I was prepared. Coach Callaghan has helped me peak at the right times, and I love the thrill of competing. I can't wait for the National Championships in February!" she exclaimed.

Michelle was in Japan in early December of the same winter for the NHK competition, another event in the Champions Series. Her first-place finish assured her a spot in the Champions Series Finals, too.

A week before Christmas, Michelle teamed up with Tara at a pro-am event, the U.S. Postal Service Challenge in the CoreStates Center in Philadelphia. For a change, they were not competing against each other. Wearing the jerseys of the hometown hockey team, the Flyers, Michelle and Tara joined skating legend Dorothy Hamill, Caryn Kadavy, and Dan Hollander in a skating competition, defeating the 76ers team, which included Nicole Bobek, Todd Eldredge, Rosalynn Sumners, and Tonia Kwiatkowski.

Tara spent part of her Christmas holiday in Los

Angeles, where she competed in an exhibition. She spread some Christmas cheer, too, when she spent an afternoon visiting sick kids at The City of Hope National Medical Center. "Tara's visit with the kids here meant so much to them. She really cheered our patients during the holidays," said Toni Carreras-Irwin, a therapist at the facility.

"I just enjoy spending time with these kids. I know how fortunate I have been and if I can share some of that with others or help them in some way, then that makes me happy," Tara commented.

At the end of the year, a poll was conducted on the Useless Skating Pages Internet web site, and skating fans were asked who they considered the favorite to win a gold medal in the 1998 Olympics. Michelle was first, followed by Chen Lu and Irina Slutskaya. Down in the eighth position out of thirteen was Tara Lipinski.

Few fans had an inkling that within a few short months, Tara would become the overwhelming favorite for Olympic gold.

8

Life off the Ice

Although the life of a competitive skater doesn't leave a lot of leisure time, both Tara and Michelle try to find some kind of balance between skating and their other interests. Being younger, Tara hadn't been on the road touring in ice shows as much as Michelle, but recently she too has stepped up her schedule of appearances.

Tara practices for about four hours a day and also takes ballet lessons off the ice. Then comes school. "I went to regular school till sixth grade," she recalled. Now she receives private tutoring. "I get a good education, one on one. Every day I do schoolwork from 3 to 7 at night. I have three tutors who come to my apartment after skating practice every day." Tara's studies include English, algebra, Spanish, history, and science. Her favorite subjects are math and biology. She also does about two hours of homework a day when she's at home.

Weekends give her more time to relax and be with her friends. "I have friends and a social life at the rink on weekends," Tara said. "I like to be with my friends and go shopping, and just relax." Her closest friend is Erin Sutton, another skater who also trains at the Detroit Skating Club.

"I like going to the mall with Erin," Tara says. "Sometimes we go to the department stores and check out what's new at cosmetic counters. Most of the time we visit our favorite store, Guess."

The two girls have sleepovers whenever their schedules allow it. They also enjoy listening to music for pleasure or to find new music to skate to. One of Tara's favorites is singer Alannis Morissette. She also likes a variety of alternative rock groups.

Tara doesn't get to watch much TV, but she enjoys shows like *Friends* and *Party of Five*. Lacey Chabert, one of the stars of *Party of Five,* is a skating fan, and after seeing Tara skate on TV, Lacey wrote Tara a letter. Tara wrote back telling the actress how much she liked the show *Party of Five*. Now the two are good friends and pen pals.

After figure skating, Tara's favorite sport to watch on TV is gymnastics. However, as far as playing other sports, Tara prefers tennis.

Tara also has several hobbies. Handy with a sewing machine, she likes to create special personalized pillows and stuffed animals—bunnies or frogs are favorites—that she designs, sews and collects. Others she gives away as gifts to friends and family. Many of Tara's friends have come to treasure her one-of-a-kind gifts.

Cooking is another favorite activity. Tara especially enjoys preparing new pasta recipes. She also loves to bake, especially chocolate cakes with chocolate frosting. Her favorite foods, she says, are spaghetti, chicken, and steak.

When she wants to concoct a sweet treat, Tara has been known to whip up a bowl of red grapes, covered with whipped cream, chocolate sprinkles, and M&Ms. "I love grapes," Tara enthused, "and chocolate-chip cookie dough ice cream."

Reading magazines is another way Tara relaxes. *Teen* and *Seventeen* are current favorites. One thing she tries to do every day is talk to her father on the phone when they are apart. Another favorite pastime is seeing movies, especially those with her favorite actor Tom Cruise.

Some of Tara's most relaxing moments are spent in her bedroom in Michigan. Her room is decorated with skating posters. One bears the motto, "The future belongs to those who believe in the beauty of their dreams," a message Tara thought about as she prepared for the 1996 Worlds. An "Ice Dreams" poster features skaters Debi Thomas, Kitty and Peter Carruthers, and several other skaters.

Tara enjoys showing visitors her jewelry collection, including her many skating necklaces that she has worn in competitions for good luck. Many of them, including the "thumbs up" necklace and the necklace that reads SHORT BUT GOOD were made by one of her uncles. Tara also loves rings, and she's been known to wear as many as eight at a time, but none when she skates.

Another of Tara's collections consists of toy frogs. Some are made of ceramics, others are stuffed animals that she has sewn herself. Tara loves animals and things with animal themes. She's been known to wear pink pig slippers that oink when they're squeezed.

Tara recently bought a computer and wants to spend more time using it. She's especially eager to read the many pieces of E-mail people have been sending to her web site. (See Tara's fact sheet at the back of this book for the web address.)

Besides skating, nothing gives Tara more pleasure than playing with her family's beloved dogs. The Lipinskis have five dogs that live at the house in Texas. There's a Yorkshire terrier named Mischief, a Maltese named Coco, a Golden Retriever, Brandy, and two Bichon Frises named Camelot and Lancelot.

Meeting her fans is important to Tara, and she especially likes to visit kids in local hospitals when she's competing or during her downtime.

Michelle's schedule is just as busy as Tara's and leaves little time for socializing or pursuing outside interests. Most of Michelle's friends are her fellow skaters at Lake Arrowhead, including Brian Boitano and Elvis Stojko. Michelle has skated with the two on several national tours and feels that now "these guys are like my older brothers," she says.

Since Karen left Lake Arrowhead to attend Boston University, Michelle has had to content herself to talking long-distance on the phone to Karen. The two still get together during holidays and when they meet at competitions. Karen has remained a world class skater, and in 1997 she finished seventh in the Nationals.

After years of being chauffeured around by her parents, Michelle couldn't wait to take her driving test and do her own driving. Trying to fit in driving practice with her skating was not easy, but she and her father spent hours in the car practicing. Michelle took the test the first time in the summer of 1996. While maneuvering around the ice is a snap for Michelle, maneuvering a car through tricky turns was not.

"I failed my first test," Michelle admitted with a laugh as she recalled the ordeal. "It was so bad. Yuck. I did a three-point turn when I wasn't supposed to. It was so scary."

Parallel parking was another fear-provoking challenge. "I've never been so nervous in my life," Michelle laughed. "Worlds was easier than taking the test. Isn't that weird? I was sweating. My hands were gripping the wheel. Driving is supposed to be easy and fun. It wasn't that day."

Karen felt sorry for her younger sister, but her brother Ron "was laughing so hard," Michelle remembered. "Everybody was. It's so embarrassing to tell anybody." Ron ribbed Michelle about flunking for weeks.

Two months later she attempted the test again, and this time she passed. Having earned more than a million dollars in 1996, she was able to afford a brand-new burnt-gold Jeep Cherokee. After she passed the test, she put a tape by singer Natalie Merchant into the car's tape deck and went out in her new car for a "victory" drive.

Michelle enjoys hopping into her car and getting away from the pressures of Lake Arrowhead. Sometimes she takes a 2½-hour drive to visit old friends in Torrance or drops in to help at the family restaurant, although there is much less time for that now.

Michelle also likes to participate in other sports besides skating. She enjoys bowling, biking, and in summer, swimming and riding her three-wheeler through the wooded areas around Lake Arrowhead. She enjoys basketball but says she only plays it for fun. "I can't do anything," she said with a laugh. "I can barely make a shot!"

Asked if she has a boyfriend, Michelle says no. The male friends she knows are all skaters and she considers them all to be just friends.

Michelle also enjoys listening to music. Some of her favorite performers are singers like Natalie Merchant, Bette Midler, and Elvis Presley.

At Lake Arrowhead, Michelle can often be found in the facility's rec room, watching TV while doing algebra or other homework. One of her favorite shows is *Family Matters*.

Michelle occasionally will fly to San Francisco, where she has special skates made for her. When she's not training, Michelle's favorite place to go is an amusement park.

Quiet time with her parents, whom Michelle calls "my heroes," is extremely important to her. "They're so much a part of me," she told an interviewer. "Without them I'd be nothing. It would be a lonely world if I didn't have my family."

Off the ice, Michelle can pass for a typical teenager. She uses very little makeup and likes to wears her hair loose. She usually prefers casual clothes, although she admits to being a "fashion freak." She adds, "I like wearing black, but I'm not trendy." When she's not on tour, Michelle likes to dress down, sometimes with a bit of a "grunge" look.

When she's traveling to competitions, Michelle enjoys wearing more stylish clothes. She loves to shop, especially when she gets to do it in foreign cities while on tour. Despite the money she's earned, Michelle is rather modest in her fashion tastes but occasionally will buy clothes by such high-fashion designers as Chanel, Gucci, and Prada. On one shopping trip in Europe she was dazzled by some Chanel suits that were selling for $10,000. She was happy just to look, but couldn't imagine spending that kind of money on a single outfit. Michelle also admires Calvin Klein designs, especially his one-shoulder dresses, and she'd love to have him design a skating outfit like that for her someday.

When she's close to home, Michelle enjoys checking out all kinds of clothing stores, trying to find sales and bargains.

Being outdoors also provides Michelle with a needed change of pace. She enjoys the wooded, mountain environment around Lake Arrowhead. She has visited Alaska, too. She's become what she calls a "fishaholic," and nothing gives her more pleasure than going on fishing trips with her dad and older brother. In the summer of 1996, while on a tour that took her to Alaska, she and two male skaters went salmon fishing. Michelle hooked a twenty-five-pound fish, and when it began fighting furiously to get away, Michelle's two male friends offered to reel it in for her. Michelle refused and landed the thrashing fish herself.

Of course, a large chunk of Michelle's time off the ice is spent doing schoolwork under the guidance of several tutors who teach her biology, English, algebra, and French. Following the 1997 Worlds, she was ready to begin the work that would make up her senior-year studies. She's thought about trying to get into Harvard and would like to go to school near Karen.

Michelle also takes classes in aerobics and ballet and even does some weight training. One of the toughest things a skater like Michelle has to deal with is keeping her weight down. She eats simply and sensibly and likes meals like chicken stir-fry. She enjoys chocolate, but because it's so fattening, she has to limit herself to an occasional small piece.

Once during her earlier training, she was allowed to eat just one piece of chocolate a month!

The life of a skater is not an easy one, and there are some who think that skaters like Tara and Michelle are missing out on a "normal life."

"A lot of people ask me that, if I missed out on a regular childhood," Michelle stated. "What have I missed? I meet new people and travel all the time. There are so many extras I've had in my life because of skating."

Tara also has no regrets. "I really don't feel I'm missing out on much," she explained. "I would never want to change it. It's hard sometimes, but it's also wonderful."

9

Trouble and Triumph
in Tennessee

There are many who consider a national championship far more challenging than the Worlds. "You're skating in front of your countrymen and everybody is attacking. The pressure is extraordinary," Dick Button, a seven-time U.S. champ and ABC-TV commentator, explained as the 1997 Nationals began in Nashville in mid-February. For a defending champion like Michelle Kwan, it would be especially tough, he predicted.

"It *is* hard to defend a national title," agreed Peggy Fleming, a five-time national champion herself. "Everyone is nipping at your heels."

During the 1996–97 skating season, Michelle Kwan seemed invincible. Since her victory in the Skate America competition in the fall of 1995, she had finished first in fourteen of fifteen events, including one pro-am event, the Ultimate Four, in which she had beaten two-time world champion Kristi Yamaguchi. Following her victory in the Honda Prelude Cup in Japan in January 1997, the *Detroit Free Press* declared, "Michelle Kwan, a year older and more mature, is almost assured of a second national championship."

As both reigning U.S. and world champion, Michelle arrived in Nashville as the overwhelming favorite. But she also came into town carrying a heavy burden—the weight of the crown and the pressure of defending it. Seven years earlier, U.S. champ Jill Trenary successfully defended her national title a second year, but no one had done it since.

"When you're defending," Michelle's coach Frank Carroll noted, "you're always looking behind you."

Like a gunfighter in the Wild West, Michelle was feeling the heat. "It's a war out there," she said. "If you don't perform, someone is going to shoot you down." Although Michelle tried to downplay the pressure, she experienced what she called "negative thoughts" for most of the week before the Nationals. In her earlier practice sessions, she said she did "about one billion triple lutzes" and didn't miss a single one. Still, she felt "a little off," she said. She was worried, nervous, and "thinking too much."

If Tara felt similar pressures, she didn't show it. Measured against the more-seasoned Michelle, Tara, the "sprite in white," as one writer dubbed her, was seen as an up-and-coming challenger whose time would come—in a few years perhaps. Tara *had* skated well the previous season and her third-place finish in the 1996 Nationals made her a real threat. But compared to Michelle's string of first-place finishes, Tara had only won a single major competition in the past season, the 1996 South Atlantic Seniors. If anyone needed a reminder of just how young Tara was, they got one when it was reported that in the week prior to the Nationals she had lost one of her baby teeth. While Tara admitted being a bit nervous, her nonchalance was a marked contrast to Michelle's doubt-filled soul-searching. Tara practiced often during the week and felt she was skating well. "I have nothing to lose," Tara stated.

On the Wednesday before the Nationals, Tara made a visit to the Vanderbilt Children's Hospital. The young patients clamored to meet her, and Tara signed autographs and shook the youngsters' hands. It was Valentine's Day, so Tara made little heart-shaped valentines and handed them out as she walked through the pediatric ward. "It makes me happy," she said, "to give a little bit back. It feels good to know I brightened someone else's day."

While Michelle often does charity work, too, her schedule in Nashville left her little time for such activities. In addition, she felt it was important to spend time with her parents. One evening prior to the competition, Michelle and her parents strolled down the Nashville streets looking in store windows.

For a few hours at least, Michelle was able to escape the pressure cooker of the Nationals. Her parents were her support system, and their presence calmed her and eased some of her doubts.

Despite all the advice to "keep cool," Tara found Friday, the day of the short program, to be a nerve-wracking one. But some of her nervousness was eased when she got a phone call from world-famous gymnastic coach Bela Karolyi. Karolyi encouraged Tara to simply skate the same way she did in practice.

Just before the start of the short program, Michelle took her final practice. A day earlier, she and her coach had changed the entrance to her triple lutz and it seemed to be giving her trouble. Michelle tried the move over and over. Her landings on a few of the jumps were rough and she took a couple of falls, but it didn't seem to concern her or her coach.

By the time Michelle and Tara took to the ice for the pre–short program warm-ups, more than 14,000 spectators had filled the Nashville Arena.

Despite her usual precompetition jitters, Tara appeared to be worry-free, as she had all week in practice. She practiced her jumps at one end of the rink, smiling each time she landed. Michelle ran through her triple jumps, too. Ominously, she fell twice during the warm-up.

"You usually don't see Michelle fall on something like this," Peggy Fleming pointed out. But Michelle had fallen in practice before and it had never affected her performances in the actual competition. However, it was an unfortunate sign of things to come for the defending champion.

Frank Carroll had a few last-minute suggestions for Michelle. "Each competition is a battle," he advised. "Be a fighter." It would be harder, he said, to defend a title than to win one for the first time. "Skate to win; don't skate not to lose," he urged.

In the short program, Michelle skated inconsistently. Dressed in a black, rhinestone-covered dress, she fell on her opening jump—a double lutz—then was unable to complete the required double toe loop that was supposed to follow. She faltered on a double lutz, but rescued it at the last second. Michelle recovered from her rough start, and the rest of her program was polished and precise. By the end, she again looked like a champion. When she finished, the crowd showered her with bouquets and stuffed animals. She received all 5.8s and 5.9s for presentation and all nine judges awarded her first-place votes, giving her a commanding lead over her competition.

"Michelle is a fighter," Frank Carroll said proudly after Michelle completed her program.

When Tara first appeared on the ice at the beginning of her short program, she looked tiny and younger than her fourteen years. In fact, more than a few spectators mistook her for one of the flower girls who collected the bouquets that fans threw onto the ice after their favorite skater performed.

Tara wore a green velvet dress with tiny buttons

and a white lace collar. If she felt any pressure at all, it did not show. "Just do your thing," Richard Callaghan advised.

Tara was focused and confident. With the eyes of the world upon her, Tara coolly nailed her triple loop, and from that moment on, it seemed that every time the camera caught her, she wore a huge smile. She didn't miss a single jump in her performance. When the final short program standings were announced, Michelle was still in first place, but Tara was right behind her, followed by Tonia Kwiatkowski.

The free skate was set for Saturday. Michelle seemed to be the focus for most of the media attention, and many in the press were still assuming—and writing—that she would win. The pressure on Michelle had started out intense and it was now building by the hour.

The hours were crawling by for Tara. She never thought Saturday would arrive, but it finally did. A few hours before the free skate program was to begin, Tara met with her coach. She was anxious and nervous.

"I'm not good enough," she told Callaghan. "I'm not going to make the world team. I don't belong here," she confessed.

"Those are all good feelings to have," her coach responded. "It's okay to be nervous. It's okay to feel that way." Reassured, Tara's moment of doubt faded away. She took a twenty-minute practice skate, then relaxed.

The free skate was a complete sellout, with more than 18,000 fans jamming the arena for the event.

As Nicole Bobek performed her program, Michelle tried to relax. She closed her eyes and concentrated on what lay ahead of her.

Nearby, Tara Lipinski, wearing a white dress with gold trim, stood and waited. A bundle of nervous energy, she shifted restlessly from skate to skate as she stood on a mat-lined walkway to the ice. Michelle and Tara would be the final two skaters in the free skate program. There was only one question now—who would end up on top, Michelle or Tara? Both skaters had ambitious programs with seven triple jumps planned. How they executed each one would spell the difference between winning and losing.

Prior to Michelle going on the ice, Carroll took her aside for a brief pep talk. "You have to skate like you're taking the castle, not defending it," he reminded her. Michelle's expression was serious and focused.

Michelle wore an elegant red-and-gold silk costume, and as the music began, Michelle seemed confident and in total control. She gradually picked up speed, then jumped high into the air to complete a graceful triple lutz–double toe combination. Her next jump was a triple lutz–triple toe loop combination, and she handled the first part with ease. But as she spun in mid-air during the second jump, it became clear that her landing would not be a smooth one. As she came down, her skate blade slipped and she fell hard. Scrambling to her feet, Michelle attempted a triple flip only to stumble on the landing. She nearly fell, and only a last-second hand on the ice prevented her from dropping to the ice again.

Michelle was shaken and seemed to have lost her composure. Trying to regain her focus and form, she began a triple loop jump, but she again lost control of her edges and toppled to the ice again. A collective groan could be heard in the stands, but most of the crowd tried to cheer Michelle on by clapping loudly in time to the music. But things continued to go badly for Michelle. She cut her final triple lutz to a double, another mishap for the now-distraught skater. Her final minute on the ice and her last jump, a triple salchow, was solid and Michelle seemed to regain her poise and focus during the rest of her program. She skated with grace and ballet-like precision, but it was too late. Michelle's mistakes had opened the door for her challengers.

Michelle tried to put on a brave face as she threw a kiss to the supportive crowd. Her sister Karen watched in dismay as Michelle left the ice to await her scores. Michelle's technical marks were not bad, ranging from 5.3 to 5.7, but they were not the marks of a champion. Michelle held back her tears, but she was clearly in distress. Her presentation marks varied from 5.6 to 5.8. They were good enough to keep her on top. But the lead was razor-thin, and Tara had yet to skate.

While she waited her turn, Tara didn't think too much about Michelle's falls. She didn't see it as important to her own skating. "I didn't have time to think, 'Oh, she didn't skate well. I have to win.' I just had to be confident and pretend it was practice," she said later.

Tara was the last skater in the free skate. As she prepared to take her warm-up skate, she huddled with her coach.

"Do your work," Callaghan instructed. "Don't try to win. Just do your work." Despite the falls, Michelle's marks had been good enough, so there would be no room for Tara to make a single mistake. She would have to land every one of her jumps to overtake Michelle. "Smile" was Callaghan's final word to Tara.

In her program, Tara planned to include an extremely difficult move that no one—male or female—had done in a competition before. She had been practicing her triple loop–triple loop combination for months and she was ready to attempt it in her long program. "I think I can do it," she told Callaghan.

As she came onto the ice, she was greeted by chants of "Tara, Tara, Tara." She skated to center ice, and buoyed by the crowd's cheers, she broke out in an excited smile. It was the moment for which she'd waited and practiced for so long. Below the stands, Jack and Pat anxiously watched Tara on a closed-circuit TV monitor.

As the music from *Sense and Sensibility* echoed through the arena, Tara began with a smooth double axel. She barely got six inches off the ice but spun so fast that she completed the move perfectly by the time she landed. Her triple flip was solid, and so were her spins and spirals. When she completed a flawless triple lutz–double toe, Tara was beaming. She knew that she was giving the performance of a lifetime.

A minute and a half later, Tara began to pick up speed in anticipation of her triple loop–triple loop, the most difficult move any skater would attempt at the Nationals. When she landed it cleanly, the audience roared its approval. Some fans began giving Tara a standing ovation even though she still had nearly a minute left. Looking as if she were having the time of her life, Tara danced in short, lively steps across the ice. By the time she ended the program with seven flying camel spins, the entire crowd was on its feet applauding. Tara wore a joyful expression as she bowed to the audience, who were loudly chanting "Six! Six! Six!"

Tara came off the ice and hugged her coaches Richard Callaghan and Megan Faulkner. Out of breath, she sat down to await her scores.

"I'm so proud of you," Callaghan told Tara.

"That was so gorgeous," Megan Faulkner raved.

Tara's technical marks were all 5.8s and 5.9s. Tara clapped her hands together in delight. The crowd whooped and hollered its approval. "Oh gosh," Tara shrieked. "I'm so happy."

When her presentation marks were announced, they were just as high, and Tara could not contain herself. "Oh my God," she exclaimed, holding her hands over her mouth. Eight judges awarded her first-place votes. Tara threw her head back exultantly and let out a wave of joyful laughter. She had just become the youngest U.S. ladies' champion of all time. Michelle was second, and Nicole Bobek third.

Tara shared the winner's podium with Michelle and Nicole and the moment was an exhilarating one. "It was as thrilling as I thought it would be," Tara said after she stepped down from the podium.

Tara unlaced her skates and met the press in her stocking feet. "I'm in shock," she said when asked how she felt. "I'm on a different wavelength. It was such a big relief after I landed the triple-triple. It was my first triple-triple in national competition. I did one one other time and I'd been practicing it a lot, so it was great when I landed it.

"When I came off the ice I didn't know I had won. I just couldn't believe it." Tara was hardly able to contain herself. "This is so exciting," she exclaimed. "I trained hard all year and my main goal was to make the world team. I just wanted to go out and do two great programs."

All eyes were on Tara. Nearby, Michelle Kwan stood off to the side talking with her coach. A sad, frustrated look covered her face.

In the men's event, Todd Eldredge won his fourth U.S. title. When he was asked what was the best part of the competition, he had a quick answer. "Watching her," he said, nodding to where Tara sat surrounded by a crowd of reporters, photographers, and TV camera crews.

The next day, even after her victory had sunk in, Tara was still surprised by the turn of events. "Today it all hit me and I love it," she said. "I was just going in there trying to do better than last year." Dressed in jeans, her light-brown hair falling loose around her shoulders, Tara looked relaxed and happy.

Richard Callaghan told the press he was absolutely convinced that Tara's skating had deserved a gold medal. But he also admitted that had Michelle skated strongly, the results might have been different.

"Michelle opened the door and Tara walked through," he explained. Callaghan was asked if he thought Tara's ascent to the top of the national skating scene might be too rapid for such a young girl.

"I want to say no," he replied. "I think Tara is bright enough to accept that she had a great night and the champion had an off night. Because Tara had a great night, she's the champion. She has a lot of years left in her career. There will be a lot of highs and lows."

Michelle Kwan showed the same grace in defeat that she had in her victories. By the next morning, she was her usual philosophical self.

"I skated like a chicken with its head cut off," she said calmly. "I guess I wasn't concentrating enough and I panicked and got scared in the middle of the performance." She shrugged and managed to smile. "I guess you have to learn to stand on that podium as well as take defeat."

Michelle was grateful to the audience who had supported her in the final minutes of her program. "I want to thank the audience for helping me out, because in the middle they started clapping, and it kind of brought me back to life.

"I know I can skate better," she added. "I have to skate better."

The Monday after the Nationals, Tara was in New York City to hit the talk show circuit. She and her mother were up at 5:45 A.M. to make an early morning taping of CBS-TV's *This Morning* and a live appearance on *Good Morning America*. Her friend and fellow champion Todd Eldredge also appeared on the show, making things more fun for Tara. The next day, Tara made a backstage visit to *Late Night with David Letterman*. Tara, a Letterman fan, loved meeting the talk show host. She also chatted with one of the guests, NASCAR driver Jeff Gordon, whose youth gave him something in common with Tara. Later, Tara and her mother took a stroll down Fifth Avenue and window-shopped.

If Tara wasn't a national celebrity before the Nationals, she was after. *People* magazine profiled her and *Sports Illustrated* hailed her as one of the brightest stars in sports. Her picture appeared on the front page of several national newspapers.

After the Nationals, Tara's own web site went online. It featured stories about Tara growing up, her life on and off the ice, and a diary where Tara records her observations and describes her travels and activities. In the month following her victory at the Nationals, more than 58,000 hits were recorded on the site.

Michelle spent the next two weeks doing a lot of soul-searching. She was shaken and plagued by doubts.

Two weeks after Nashville, the Champions Series Finals took place in Hamilton, Ontario. The event was an Olympic-style event featuring the best skaters in the world. It was the climax to a series of competitions that took place in the United States, Canada, Russia, Japan, and the Soviet Union. As the Finals got underway in the Copps Coliseum, the event was seen as Michelle's chance to regain her form and reestablish herself as the favorite in the upcoming Worlds in Lausanne, Switzerland. Tara, along with American Tonia Kwiatkowski and Russian champion Irina Slutskaya, were also scheduled to compete in the event. Sweetening the stakes was a $50,000 first prize.

"I want to show everybody that I've still got it," Michelle stated. Her hair hung loose and without makeup she looked youthful, but there was a determined look in her eyes.

"This is a fight," she declared. "It's a war." The skater who had stumbled at the Nationals had been banished, Michelle said. "It was like someone took over my body and skated for me. I've thrown her away. She doesn't live anymore."

"I'm not expecting to win or place," Tara said modestly. "I just want to do my best."

In the short program, Michelle skated first, and

she struggled from the start. On her opening combination jump, she fell to the ice hard. Failing to complete the required move would cost her crucial points. Michelle rallied to finish her program in better form, but the mistake had lowered her scores.

"Maybe I was thinking too much of the perfect takeoff," she said afterwards. "I missed it, I guess. I had a lot of power and confidence. I was very surprised to be [down] on the ice."

Tara again seized the opportunity. Despite a less-than-perfect takeoff on her triple lutz–double loop, she skated her entire program without error and with plenty of grace and style. The crowd rose to its feet and gave her an ovation after she completed a triple lutz–double loop combination and triple toe loop. Wearing an exuberant smile, Tara finished with a superb set of spins. Five of the judges ranked her first, but several judges gave her less-than-spectacular technical scores. The crowd, clearly behind Tara, booed loudly as those scores were announced.

"I really didn't care about the marks," Tara said after. "I know I did the best I could have done."

When the final results for the short program were tallied, Tara was in first, followed by Russia's Maria Butyrskaya and Michelle in third. Michelle knew the long program lay ahead, and since it was worth two-thirds of the total, she could easily make a comeback.

"I have to go for all of the jumps with the eye of a tiger," she vowed.

Jumps were the name of the game in the free skate. Tara had a shaky opening, two-footing her landing and almost skidding into the sideboards on a botched double axel. But she quickly recovered and landed all seven of her triple jumps cleanly, including the triple loop–triple loop she had unveiled at Nashville.

Michelle, skating last, started strong with two perfect triple-triple combinations. But then she faltered. On a triple loop, she had to reach down to the ice to steady herself, and on another triple jump, she stumbled as she landed. Michelle's artistry was evident throughout her program, however, and three of the judges ranked her first. Four declared Tara tops.

Once again, the short program had been critical. Tara won the competition and the $50,000 first-prize money.

"I'm shocked, surprised," said Tara. "I knew there was money, but I didn't know it was that much.

"This was great. The Nationals were great," Tara added excitedly, "but we have to take it day to day."

Michelle, on the other hand, was unnerved by her showing, but trying to make the best of it. "It's not one of my best performances," she admitted, "but I'll take it for now." Her confidence, she admitted, "was not very high, a 7 of 10. But it's getting better. After the Nationals, it was a 1, almost a negative 1.

"It's not the end of the world," Michelle continued hopefully. "I've still got the Worlds."

10

On to the Olympics

Up until the 1997 Nationals, Richard Callaghan was optimistic that Tara would have a chance for an Olympic gold medal—at the 2002 Winter Games in Salt Lake City, Utah. With Tara's triumph at the 1997 Worlds, he now had to rethink their goals. Tara was now the favorite for Olympic gold, not in 2002, but in 1998 in Nagano, Japan.

Tara's victory in Lausanne had made her a superstar seemingly overnight. It also opened the floodgates for all kinds of commercial endorsement offers. Following the Worlds, Tara was recruited by a Canadian company that wanted her to wear their skating costumes. She was offered a million-dollar book deal to publish her autobiography. There were discussions about fashion deals with designer

Donna Karan. A toy company even pitched a line of Tara Lipinski dolls to her management.

In addition, Tara was invited to join the Campbell's Soups Tour of World Figure Skating Champions, which hit the road after the Worlds. Some of the biggest names in skating were featured in the show. Tara and Michelle were among them, along with Elvis Stojko, the 1997 men's world champion, Olympic medal winners Nancy Kerrigan and Oksana Baiul, and Brian Boitano, recently named a 1997 Figure Skating Hall of Fame inductee. The tour drew sellout crowds in cities across the country. Tara appeared in forty-five of the sixty-plus shows in the tour and earned close to $225,000. Michelle skated in even more shows, and her earnings for the year would again top $1 million. Both skaters won rave reviews for their elegant skating and enchanting performances.

It was times like those that reminded Michelle of all the great moments she's had in her career. "Sometimes," she explained, "you step on the ice and it's just awesome. It's like you were born on skates."

On April Fool's Day Michelle made an appearance on *The Tonight Show* with Jay Leno. Dressed casually in black tapered pants and a simple black jacket, Michelle seemed quite at ease as she joked with Leno. He asked Michelle how she felt about Tara and Michelle replied that they were friends off the ice and competitors on it. Later, Leno asked Michelle to demonstrate one of her jumps on "dry land." Michelle agreed, but told Leno "only if you do it after me!" Michelle did a quick double axel, then she and the audience cracked up as Leno whirled around with one leg sticking out awkwardly. The crowd loved it, and Leno asked Michelle to return to the show in the future.

Tara also received offers to be on TV talk shows. She was most excited by an invitation to be on Rosie O'Donnell's show. Tara was thrilled to be Rosie's guest. Tara and Rosie had met earlier in the year and had enjoyed each other's company and shared jokes about Tara's favorite actor, Tom Cruise.

Soon after, Michelle appeared in another skating event, the Hershey's Kisses Skating Challenge. She skated to "Just Around the River Bend" from *Pocahantas*. Michelle was clearly back in top form, and she received several perfect 6.0s for her performances. In July, she teamed up with her friend and fellow champion Brian Boitano for "Skating Romance III." The show was a special one-time performance in Atlantic City and Boitano personally chose Michelle as his co-star.

Both Michelle and Tara enjoyed skating in these shows, since they provided a release from the pressure of events like the Nationals and Worlds.

The competition in figure skating is always fierce, and because of all the media attention, it often seemed as if there were a strong rivalry between the two skaters. Both Tara and Michelle know that there can only be one gold medal winner in ladies' figure skating in Nagano, but they do not really consider themselves "rivals." In fact, they are friendly. "We talk off the ice, in the locker room," Tara said. "It's just normal, outside-of-skating things. Nothing about skating."

Of Michelle's difficulties, Tara says, "Everyone has a point where they come down a little, and they come back up. I don't think it's a rivalry."

Michelle does consider Tara to be a rival, but only on the ice. Otherwise, her relationship with Tara is a friendly one.

Following their touring, both skaters began their training for the next season. Tara and her coach have toyed with the idea of adding a quad jump, a move that no other woman skater has done in competition. Or they may add a triple axel, which in women's skating has only been done by two women skaters, Tonya Harding and Midori Ito.

Michelle also plans to make changes in her program. She knows she has the abilities to win a gold medal, but it's her mental attitude she wants to work on. Her main focus for the 1997–98 season is to keep her confidence level high and learn from her mistakes. "This year I put a lot of pressure on myself," she said. "I got focused on the wrong thing, and I learned my lesson."

Conquering her fear was something Michelle knew she had to do after the Worlds, and her performances in the off-season helped her do that. Recalling how in Nashville she skated like "a chicken with its head cut off," Michelle now says she's gotten things back together. "The chicken is gone," she joked. "I killed it."

Her coach confirmed Michelle's statement. "I think Michelle had a very big lesson to learn this year," Carroll said. "When you are champion, you have to fight and come out like it's a whole new battle. Despite the fact that I explained it to her, I think she was still thinking she was champion. I feel already her attitude will be different next year."

As the world champion, Tara was suddenly considered the top candidate to win the gold medal at Nagano. Did that, she was asked, put a lot of pressure on her?

"Not really," Tara answered cheerfully, "because if I put it in perspective, I know what I have to do out there. It's only my first Olympics and I'm just gonna go for it. If I make the team, I'll be happy."

Of course, like any skater, Tara's future is uncertain. Anything can happen. A growth spurt can wreak havoc on a skater's style, especially her jumps.

Tara's small size, some say, gives her an advantage over Michelle, who at age sixteen was six inches taller and twenty-five pounds heavier than Tara. As a skater gets older and gains weight, it can become more difficult to perform with the same style and grace one did earlier. Sometimes even just a little weight gain can throw off a skater's timing or prevent her from completing all the mid-air revolutions required in a jump.

"Obviously, when you're smaller, things are a lot

easier," said Todd Eldredge. "When you start to grow, things can change."

Tara really isn't worried about that. "I know I'll be able to handle it," she said. "I've been growing forever. If I keep up with my training and programs, I think it will be okay."

Tara's doctors have said she's not likely to grow that much more, so that may not be a problem. But in a demanding sport like figure skating, an injury can end a career completely.

Tara also knows that every year, talented newcomers will come along and vie for the title. "You can't stay on top forever. I don't think anyone can finish first every year," she said. "Next year I'd love to be first, but my main goal is to be on the world team. Just being a champion, no matter what the age, is great."

Pat Lipinski thinks her daughter is prepared for both winning and losing. "If it ended tomorrow," Pat Lipinski asked, "know what she'd say? 'I'd start something else.'"

For now, the 1998 and the 2002 Winter Games are on the horizon, and both Tara and Michelle are focused on an Olympic gold.

"The Olympics are my goal," Tara declared. "Any Olympics would be fine. I haven't really thought about which one. My dream has always been to win the Olympics."

"Tara wants the Olympics. She wants gold," Richard Callaghan echoed. "And she will make it happen."

"She always rises to the occasion," Jack Lipinski agreed.

Tara can even envision competing against Michelle in the 2002 Winter Games. Michelle will be just twenty-one, while Tara will be nineteen. "If she's going to stay around," Tara suggested, "I guess I'll have to beat her."

Michelle has her heart set on the Olympics, too. "I've always dreamed about going to the Olympics and seeing the Olympic rings," she stated. It's been a goal she's had ever since she watched Brian Boitano win a gold medal ten years earlier.

Michelle can also see her and Tara competing "for the next twenty-five years," she said. "We're both young. I don't know how long she intends to be skating, but I'll be there always."

And if Michelle doesn't win? As usual, she is willing to accept the possibility. "I guess I'll be disappointed," she admitted. "But you have to learn to cope and be happy and enjoy life. A lot of things aren't going to go your way."

At the same time, Michelle's ambitions go beyond the Olympics. "I want to be a legend like Dorothy Hamill and Peggy Fleming. I want to leave a little mark, and have people say 'Michelle Kwan was a great skater, artistically and technically. She had the whole package.' I want people to remember me after 1,000 years when skating is weird and people are doing quintuple jumps," she told the *New York Times*.

Frank Carroll is quick to advise everyone that

Michelle is a champion and cannot be counted out, no matter what difficulties she may have had during the winter of 1997. "Michelle has a core of metal," he warned. "She is as tough as nails."

Both Tara's and Michelle's coaches are quick to compliment the other skater.

"I think they're both wonderful," says Frank Carroll. "Right now you're looking at two different styles. One is turning easy, jumping easy. The other is more experienced, more limber, more to the music, more able to give something from the heart."

"They're both great champions," agrees Richard Callaghan. "It just depends on who's better on a particular day."

Tara Lipinski—Competitive History

Competition	Place
1997 Championships Series Final	1st
1997 National Senior	1st
1996 U.S. Postal Service Challenge (team)	1st
1996 Nations Cup	2nd
1996 Trophy Lalique	3rd
1996 Skate Canada	2nd
1996 World Championships	15th
1996 National Senior	3rd
1996 South Atlantic Senior	1st
1996 World Junior Championship	5th
1996 World Junior Selections Competition	2nd
1995 Nebelhorn Trophy	4th
1995 National Junior	2nd
1995 World Junior Championships	4th
1994 Blue Swords	1st
1994 U.S. Olympic Festival	1st

Competition	Place
1994 National Novice	2nd
1994 Midwestern Novice	1st
1994 Southwestern Novice	1st

Tara Lipinski Fact Sheet

Born: June 10, 1982, Philadelphia, PA
Height: 4' 8" Weight: 78 lbs.
Home Club: Detroit Skating Club
Hometown: Sugar Land, Texas
Training Town: Bloomfield Hills, Michigan
Coaches: Richard Callaghan, Megan Faulkner
Hobbies: Cooking, sewing, making stuffed animals and pillows, listening to music
Favorite Activities (other than skating): Tennis, swimming, hanging out with friends
Favorite Color: Purple
Favorite Food: Pasta
Favorite Book: *All Things Great and Small*
Favorite Animal: Dogs
Favorite Athletes: Dominique Moceanu, Todd Eldredge, Kristi Yamaguchi
Ambitions: To win a gold medal at Nagano; to become a lawyer
Web Site Address: www.taralipinski.com

Michelle Kwan—Competitive History

Competition	Place
1997 World Championships	2nd
1997 Championship Series Final	2nd
1997 National Senior	2nd
1997 Japan Open	1st
1997 Ultimate Four	1st
1996 U.S. Postal Service Challenge (team)	1st
1996 Trophy Lalique	1st
1996 Thrifty Car Rental Skate America	1st
1996 The Continents Cup	1st
1996 Hershey's Kisses Challenge (team)	1st
1996 World Championships	1st
1996 Championships Series Final	1st
1996 Centennial on Ice	3rd
1996 National Senior	1st
1995 U.S. Postal Service Challenge (team)	1st
1995 Nations Cup	1st

Competition	Place
1995 Skate Canada	1st
1995 Skate America	1st
1995 World Team Challenge	4th
1995 Hershey's Kisses International Challenge	1st
1995 World Championships	4th
1995 National Senior	2nd
1994 Thrifty Car Rental International Challenge	3rd
1994 Trophy de France	3rd
1994 Skate America	2nd
1994 U.S. Outdoor Challenge	1st
1994 Goodwill Games	2nd
1994 Hershey's Kisses Pro-Am Championships	1st
1994 World Championships	8th
1994 National Senior	2nd
1994 World Junior Championships	1st
1993 Skate America	7th
1993 U.S. Olympic Festival	1st
1993 Gardena Spring Trophy	1st
1993 National Senior	6th
1993 Pacific Coast Senior	1st
1993 Southwest Pacific Senior	1st
1992 National Junior	9th
1992 Pacific Coast Junior	3rd
1992 Southwest Pacific Junior	1st

Michelle Kwan Fact Sheet

Born: July 7, 1980, Torrance, California
Height: 5′ 2″ Weight: 100 lbs.
Home Club: Los Angeles Figure Skating Club
Hometown: Torrance, California
Training Town: Lake Arrowhead, California
Coach: Frank Carroll
Hobbies: Shopping
Favorite Activities (other than skating): Swimming, bowling, biking, basketball, riding her three-wheeler, hanging out with friends at Lake Arrowhead
Favorite Colors: Turquoise and black
Favorite Foods: Lasagna, pizza
Favorite Book: *Night* by Elie Wiesel
Favorite Animal: Monkey (Michelle's Chinese calendar sign is the monkey.)
Favorite Athlete: Michael Jordan
Ambition: To win an Olympic gold medal at Nagano, Japan

Glossary of Skating Terms

Axel jump. One of the most difficult jumps, in which a skater takes off from the forward outside edge and lands on the back outside edge of the opposite foot. A single axel consists of 1½ revolutions, a double is 2½ revolutions, and a triple is 3½ revolutions. Named for its inventor Axel Paulsen, it is easily recognizable as the only jump that takes off from a forward position.

Camel spin. A spin that is done on one leg with the nonskating leg, or free leg, extended in the air in a position parallel to the ice. The body remains in the "spiral" position while spinning.

Combination spin. The combination of several spins where the skater changes feet and positions while maintaining speed throughout the entire spin.

Crossovers. A method of gaining speed and turning corners in which skaters cross one foot over the other.

Edges. The two sides of the skate blade on either side of a grooved center. There is an inside edge on the inner side of the leg and an outside edge that is on the outside of the leg. There is a forward and a backward for each edge, equaling four different edges.

Edge jump. A jump where the skater takes off from the entry edge of the skating foot without bringing the free foot in contact with the ice to assist the takeoff. The axel, loop, and salchow are edge jumps.

Flip jump. A toe pick–assisted jump, taken off from the back edge of one foot and landed on the back outside edge of the opposite foot.

Footwork. A sequence of step maneuvers carrying the skater across the ice in patterns, generally straight, circular, or serpentine. Footwork is intended to show the precision and dexterity of the skater's movements.

Free skate. The free skate counts for 66.7% of a skater's or a team's final score. It doesn't have any required elements. Senior-level free skate time is 4½ minutes for men and pairs, 4 minutes for women.

Layback spin. Generally performed by women, the layback spin involves an upright spin position where the head and shoulders are dropped backwards and the back arches.

Long program. Slang term for the free skating portion of the singles and pairs competition.

Loop jump. An edge jump, taken off from a back outside edge and landed on the same back outside edge.

Lutz jump. A toe pick–assisted jump, taken off from a back outside edge and landed on the back outside edge of the opposite foot. The skater glides backwards on a curve, taps the toe pick into the ice, and rotates in the opposite direction of the curve. Named after its inventor Alois Lutz.

Presentation mark. The second of two marks awarded when judging the singles and pairs short program and free skate. Judges consider the program's relationship to the music, the speed, utilization of ice surface, carriage, style, and originality.

Regionals. The first of two qualifying competitions en route to the U.S. Championships. Skaters must place in the top four to qualify.

Required element marks. The first mark given by the judges in the singles and pairs short programs, evaluating how well each element is performed.

Salchow. An edge jump, taken off from the back inside edge of one foot and landed on the back outside edge of the opposite foot.

Sectionals. The second and final qualifying competition en route to the U.S. Championship. The top four finishers go onto the Championships.

Short program. Official name for a two-minute, forty-second program in singles and pairs that consists of eight required elements and is set to the skater's music of choice. No more than eight elements are allowed, and failure to perform an element results in penalty of points.

Sit spin. A spin that is done in a "sitting" position. The body is low to the ice with the sitting (spinning) knee bent and the nonskating "free" leg extended behind it.

Spiral. A move in which a skater demonstrates flexibility and a fluid line by extending her nonskating leg behind her into the air during a long glide.

Spiral sequence. A sequence of steps that incorporates various spirals in a pattern across the ice. Spirals in a spiral sequence may be done going forward, backwards, in a straight line, or on a curve, on an inside or outside edge.

Starting order. The result of the draw, which lists the order in which the skaters will compete and the group in which each skater will warm up prior to competition.

Step sequence. A sequence of steps that immediately follow one another, executed in time to the music and choreographically related to each other.

Technical merit mark. The first of two marks awarded when judging the free skate. It measures the difficulty, variety, and cleanness of the performance.

Toe loop. A toe pick–assisted jump that takes off and lands on the same back outside edge.

Toe picks. The teeth at the front of the blade, used primarily for jumping and spinning.

About the Author

Chip Lovitt is the author of more than three dozen children's books, including *Inventions No One Mentions, The Great Rock 'n' Roll Photo Quiz Book, The Ultimate Disney Joke Book* and a variety of sports books including biographies of Michael Jordan, Charles Barkley, Magic Johnson, and Nancy Kerrigan. He lives in New Milford, Connecticut, with his son, Keith.

@café

Meet the staff of @café:
Natalie, Dylan, Blue, Sam, Tanya, and Jason.
They serve coffee, surf the net,
and share their deepest darkest secrets . . .

A brand-new book series coming in November 1997

#1 Love Bytes
It's not just the espresso
that's brewing. . . .

#2 I'll Have What He's Having
It's not the caffeine
that's making everyone jumpy.

Novels by Elizabeth Craft

Available from Archway Paperbacks
Published by Pocket Books

POCKET
BOOKS

1430

Have you ever wished for the complete guide to surviving your teenage years? At long last, here's your owner's manual—a book of instructions and insights into exactly how YOU operate.

LET'S TALK ABOUT ME!

A Girl's Personal, Private, and Portable Instruction Book for life

Learn what makes boys so weird
Discover the hidden meanings in your doodles
Uncover the person you want to be
Get to know yourself better than anyone else
Laugh a little
Think a little
Grow a little

TOP-SECRET QUIZZES, COOL ACTIVITIES, AND MUCH MORE

Being a teenage girl
has never been so much fun!

FROM THE CREATORS OF
THE BESTSELLING CD-ROM!

An Archway Paperback
Published by Pocket Books

1433

party of five™

Join the party!

**Read these new books
based on the hit TV series.**

#1 Bailey:
On My Own

#2 Julia:
Everything Changes

Available mid-October

POCKET
BOOKS

From Archway Paperbacks
Published by Pocket Books